Dwight Longenecker

SLUBGRIP INSTRUCTS
Fifty Days with the Devil

SLUBGRIP INSTRUCTS

Fifty Days with the Devil

Dwight Longenecker

STAUFFER
BOOKS

STAUFFER BOOKS
Terra Lane, Greenville, SC

COVER ART
Christopher J. Pelicano

BOOK DESIGN
Christopher J. Pelicano and Abby Glazier

PRINTED AND BOUND IN THE U.S.A
Color House Graphics

ISBN 978-0-9862713-0-4

Contents

Foreword   i

Cast of Characters   v

Introduction   vii

Letter from His Eminence, Thornblade, DMn   1

WEEK OF ASH WEDNESDAY

Shrove Tuesday	3
Ash Wednesday	4
Thursday	7
Friday	9
Saturday	11

FIRST WEEK OF LENT

Sunday	13
Monday	15
Tuesday	17
Wednesday	19
Thursday	21
Friday	23
Saturday	25

SECOND WEEK OF LENT

Sunday	29
Monday	30
Tuesday	32
Wednesday	34
Thursday	36
Friday	38
Saturday	40

Contents

THIRD WEEK OF LENT

Sunday	43
Monday	45
Tuesday	48
Wednesday	50
Thursday	52
Friday	54
Saturday	56

FOURTH WEEK OF LENT

Sunday	59
Monday	61
Tuesday	64
Wednesday	66
Thursday	68
Friday	71
Saturday	74

FIFTH WEEK OF LENT

Sunday	77
Monday	79
Tuesday	81
Wednesday	83
Thursday	86
Friday	88
Saturday	90

Contents

PASSION WEEK

Palm Sunday	93
Monday	96
Tuesday	98
Wednesday	100
Maundy Thursday	102
Good Friday	104
Holy Saturday	106

EASTER

Easter Sunday	111
Easter Monday	114

by Dr. Devin Brown

On a pleasant spring day in 1941, British readers opened *The Guardian*, an Anglican religious newspaper, to find the first in a series of strange letters. Beginning on May 2nd and then every week afterwards for thirty-one weeks, another of these mysterious letters would be printed, each claiming to have been written by a senior devil named Screwtape to his nephew, a novice tempter named Wormwood. The entire collection was released in Britain in 1942 and in the United States a year later as *The Screwtape Letters*.

Though he had published four books previously—*The Pilgrim's Regress* (1933), *The Allegory of Love* (1936), *Out of the Silent Planet* (1938), and *The Problem of Pain* (1940)—as well as numerous works of poetry, *The Screwtape Letters* would go on to become Lewis's breakout book. With *Mere Christianity* (1952) and *The Chronicles of Narnia* (1950-1956), works for which he is now better known, not to come until nearly a decade later, it was *The Screwtape Letters* that first propelled Lewis to international fame and eventually put him on the cover of Time magazine on September 8, 1947—where he was pictured with a little devil standing on one shoulder.

The *Time* cover story "Don versus Devil," a reference to Lewis's position as an Oxford don, noted that by 1947 all of Lewis's books added together had sold something over a million copies. Today the number of copies of *Screwtape* alone stands at many million.

The origins for the series of devilish epistles can be found in a letter which Lewis wrote to his brother Warnie dated July 20, 1940. In it Lewis writes:

> *I have been to Church for the first time for many weeks owing to the illness.... Before the service was over—one could wish these things came more seasonably—I was struck by an idea for a book which I think might be both useful and entertaining. It would be called* As One Devil to Another *and would consist of letters from an elderly retired devil to a young devil who has just started work on his first "patient." The idea would be to give*

all the psychology of temptation from the other point of view.

Unlike his close friend J. R. R. Tolkien who often required years to complete a major writing project, it did not take Lewis long to both finish and find a publisher for *Screwtape*, with the first installment appearing in *The Guardian* less than nine months after the letter to Warnie. Lewis dedicated the book to J. R. R. Tolkien, who during a late night walk on a warm September evening had played an important role in leading him to Christ—so important that it could be claimed that without Tolkien's influence there may have never been a *Screwtape*.

In the fourth book of *Paradise Lost*, Milton has Satan declare, "Evil, be thou my good," and a similar reversal of perspective is seen throughout *Screwtape*. As Lewis scholar Mark DeForrest has pointed out, an awareness of this other point of view used by Lewis is crucial to understanding the content of the letters. Thus, readers find that the Enemy in the story is Screwtape's way of referring to God, and what Screwtape calls Our Father's House is of course, Hell, not Heaven. DeForrest concludes, "It is necessary to keep in mind that what Screwtape sees as good is really negative, and what are setbacks for him are actually victories in the struggle against evil." Or as Jocelyn Easton Gibb puts it in the Preface to "Screwtape Proposes a Toast," Screwtape's whites are our blacks and those things he welcomes we should dread.

One would think this point hardly needed mentioning. However in the Preface to the 1961 edition of *Screwtape*, Lewis relates the story of the country clergyman who wrote a letter to the editor canceling his subscription to *The Guardian* complaining that much of the advice given in the letters seemed "not only erroneous but positively diabolical."

Lewis choose to begin *The Screwtape Letters* with two epigraphs. The first is advice from Martin Luther: "The best way to drive out the devil, if he will not yield to texts of Scripture, is to jeer and flout him, for he cannot bear scorn." The second epigraph is a line quoted from Thomas More describing the Devil as a proud spirit who "cannot endure to be mocked." In choosing to open with these quotes, Lewis reveals his own intentions to use satire and ridicule as a means of pointing out and overcoming the Devil's snares. In *Slubgrip Instructs: Fifty Days with the Devil*, Father Dwight Longenecker continues in this same tradition with a book that is both delightful and insightful, one whose colorful characters (Slubgrip, Grimwort, Snozzle, Snort, and others) will both entertain and—in their unique backwards way—provide useful instruction.

Of the many influences which the Catholic writer G. K. Chesterton had on Lewis, one of the greatest was the central importance which Chesterton placed on humor and laughter. In the Preface to the 1961 edition of *Screwtape*, Lewis refers to the line in Orthodoxy where Chesterton suggests that Satan fell by "the force of gravity." Lewis then observes: "We must picture Hell as a state where everyone is perpetually concerned about his own dignity and advancement, where everyone has a grievance, and where everyone lives the deadly serious passions of envy, self-importance, and resentment." By contrast, as Chesterton points out in the same section of *Orthodoxy*, "A characteristic of great saints is their power of levity. Angels can fly because they can take themselves lightly." Readers will find the devilish machinations recounted in *Slubgrip Instructs* to be the perfect antidote for those times when they are tempted to get caught up in their own self-importance and schemes for self-advancement and are in need a mirror to show them the truth behind these deceptions.

Though told from a devil's point of view, *Screwtape* remains essentially an uplifting book. In spite of the impressive array of tactics employed by the forces of darkness, the young man's faith in Christ triumphs in the end and serves as an example of how ordinary Christians can find similar success in their own lives. So, too, Slubgrip Instructs—in its indirect, reverse way—reveals the glorious victory of the rabbi from Nazareth.

Lewis claimed that *Screwtape* was an unpleasant book to for him to write and despite requests for additional correspondence from Screwtape he felt "not the least inclination" to write any more. "Though I had never written anything more easily, I never wrote with less enjoyment," Lewis explained. "The work into which I had to project myself while I spoke through Screwtape was all dust, grit, thirst, and itch." In the end readers had to content themselves with only one addition short piece from Lewis called "Screwtape Proposes a Toast" which appeared in *The Saturday Evening Post* on December 19, 1959.

With the publication of *Slubgrip Instructs: Fifty Days with the Devil*, Father Longenecker serves up a delicious series of devilish lectures to Lewis fans who have been hungry for more accounts of temptation from this other point of view.

Perhaps because it was the first of his books with huge public success, Lewis always seemed ready to poke fun at the notoriety that

The Screwtape Letters enjoyed. In the 1961 Preface, he refers to it as the sort of book that is "given to godchildren" and then "gravitates towards spare bedrooms, there to live a life of undisturbed tranquility in company with *The Road Mender, John Inglesant,* and *The Life of the Bee.*" It is highly unlikely that *The Screwtape Letters* has ever or will ever be placed in the same category as any of these largely forgotten works, and now *Slubgrip Instructs: Fifty Days with the Devil* proudly takes its place alongside it.

Devin Brown
English Department
Asbury University

CAST OF CHARACTERS

Slubgrip	Professor of Popular Culture, Bowelbages University
Grimwort	Associate Professor of Popular Culture, Bowelbages University
Thornblade	President, Bowelbages University
Knobswart	Friend of Slubgrip; Professor of Fraud and Finance, Bowelbages University
Crasston	Commissioner of Security, Bowelbages University
Snozzle	Director, Department of Detention, Bowelbages University
Snort, Slurge, Shanklin	Students in Popular Culture 101

GUEST LECTURERS

Zelnick	Professor of Film Studies, Bowelbages University
Starlow	Retired Temptress; Author, *Sirens and Seduction*
Karmeleon	Professor of Eastern Religions, Bowelbages University
Swagger	Active Tempter, Religion Department SouthEast
Gecko	Active Tempter, Finance and Fraud Division NorthEast
Snoot	Active Tempter; Founder, Materialism and Malice International
Strump	Professor of Gender Studies, Bowelbages University
Flambeaux	Associate Professor of Gender Studies, Bowelbages University
Claxton	Senior Tempter, Politics and Passion, NorthEast
Dowdy	Professor of Media Studies, Bowelbages University
Oskar Fullmann	Professor of New Testament Criticism, Bowelbages University
Starfox	Director of the Institute for Occult Science, Bowelbages University

A Letter to the Reader

From the Seventh Celestial Circle

Children of the Covenant,

Greetings in the name of the Highest! All blessings to you from the Father of Light. May you know the powerful purity of her who has crushed the dragon's head, and the joy of all your brothers and sisters in the celestial realm.

Gentle children, before you begin reading these dark deceptions we wish you to hear our words of instruction. We have carefully recorded these lectures from the fallen ones and composed them in a manner for you to read during the Forty Days of Testing. The words of the dark lords may be read at any time, but it is best to begin on the day before the Wednesday of Ashes and continue daily to the celebration of the Rising of the World's True Life.

What you read here may disturb you. The smoke and stench of hell itself reeks in these pages, and it was much debated among us whether it should be released to you at all.

However, the times are so perilous and the battle so intense that it was decided that it is better for you to observe the actions and intentions of the dark ones than to fall into the trap of neglecting their wiles and forgetting their existence. They flourish when you do not believe in them. They love nothing more than for you to be complacent, negligent and lazy.

Remember, dear ones, the servants of the Dark love to hide. Camouflage and subterfuge are their clothing. As you read, you will find yourself entwined in a web of deception and counter-deception.

You may feel soiled by the Enemy's vulgarity and sickened by his coarse speech. You may become despondent at the complexity of the Enemy's plan. You may become confused by his strategies and bewildered by his chicanery.

When this happens, look to the light. One moment of honest prayer and adoration will open the windows of your soul. Look upward to the clear, fresh breeze of the North. Instantly you will be given the childlike simplicity that your soul requires. At once you will see what you should do. Then ask for the grace to run from the darkness into the light.

It is therefore with a mixture of joy and concern that we share with you the teachings of one of our fallen members, Slubgrip. His name before the Great Rebellion was "Shaddiel." How glorious a servant of Light was Shaddiel! His radiance was noble and his words had the sweetness of honey; his song was like the soft light of the moon and the hard beauty of diamonds. He bore in his manner and his speech the double gift of humor and humility. Oh, Shaddiel, how are you fallen!

Learn from them, dear children of the covenant. Turn while you can to the Father of Light and rejoice in the triumph of the resurrected One. Rejoice with us in the Unity of the Three, and join your hearts with the Blessed Lady and that great cloud of witnesses who circle around the throne with songs of everlasting joy.

Your guardian and guide

Bowelbages University

Learn to Burn, Burn to Learn

◆

Memo:
From: His Eminence, Thornblade, DMn
       President and Director of Communications
       Department of Infernal Security
       Re-Education Division

To: Heads of Department - Bowelbages University

CONFIDENTIAL

Diabolical Doctors,

It has come to our attention that there has been a dangerous lapse in security. Our surveillance systems have been compromised, and transcripts of lectures and conversations have fallen into enemy hands.

Be reminded that you are responsible for all listening devices, drones, security cameras, two-way mirrors, monitoring systems and third-party observation technologies.

The worst leaks have been from chamber 101 in which Slubgrip lectures on Popular Culture. Serious leaks have also emanated from *The Lavatory Coffee Shoppe* where he meets for lava and larva.

Commissioner Crasston has instructed the Flancks to conduct the search for rogue listening devices after

Bowelbages University

Learn to Burn, Burn to Learn

◆

hours, and Professor Slubgrip is not to be informed of the security breach. Our Father Below has reason to believe that there is more to this security problem than meets the eye. Serious cyber sabotage is suspected, with the possibility that Slubgrip may be plotting a coup within the administrative structures of the University.

Until the enquiries are complete, you are to conduct yourselves as normal with Slubgrip and ensure that all security devices for which you are responsible are properly serviced as per chapter seventeen, article forty three of the Bowelbages University Management and Manipulation Manual.

Be on the alert. Remember Our Father Below is watching.

Sincerely,

Thornblade

DAY ONE ~ *Shrove Tuesday*

Slubgrip's Lair

Door opening. A deep cultured voice is heard. It is Slubgrip.

Ah, Knobswart you old reptile, come in, come in. How have the mighty fallen, eh? That we should both be reduced to this—teaching these scrofulous slugs the ABCs of tempting! I suppose we must reconcile ourselves to the long, slow ascent, but it is tiresome—this never-ending cycle of clawing one's way back to the top, only to slip up and find oneself flushed back into the lowest levels of existence.

I never imagined for a moment that I would be so betrayed, and that my honorary dinner would result in my own consumption. I hear your invitation to dinner soon followed. The only good thing about my sentence to teach in this infernal university is that you and I might meet again as equals. Did I say "equals," Knobswart? Of course I didn't mean "equal" in ability. You have always been my superior by far! By "equal" I meant "colleague" or "comrade in arms"!

Will you have a drink, my old friend? I've been keeping a bottle of red for a special occasion. This red happens to be Lenin '24. Why not share a glass with me for old times' sake? Do you know what day this is? It's Shrove Tuesday—Fat Tuesday I like to call it. Do you know that fool Dogswart—who was one of my students—once got his young patient to overindulge at a Mardi Gras party and thought he'd scored points? The boy just went off to an Ash Wednesday service the next day and "got religion" for the first time, so the end result was worse than the first.

This tempting business is not as easy as they think. Happily you and I have the experience to see that. How manifestly unfair that we should have been so demoted and betrayed! It wasn't my fault that a few things went wrong. I was misinformed! My enemies plotted and brought me down, and I'm determined to get my own back. You'll see!

This has got me thinking, Knobby, and I'm convinced that you and I need not remain in such lowly positions here at Bowelbages. With a bit of ingenuity we may find a way of advancement that would be pleasing to both of us. I've had an idea and I wonder what you think.

I don't know how you feel about it, but I was particularly amazed, and I must say, disgusted, to find that first Thornblade had been appointed as Director of Communications, and now he is titling himself as "President." I was also completely astounded to find Crasston and Snozzle as Commissioner of Security and Head of the Department of Detention. How Thornblade could appoint two such mediocre and incompetent tempters to such responsible posts I have no idea.

Now then Knobby, my idea is that we might form a team. Why shouldn't you be President of Bowelbages and perhaps I might take over from Crasston and Snozzle? Security and Detention ought to be a combined role anyway.

If Thornblade's authority were undermined—let's say with a student revolt along with some unpleasant news being released about Crasston and Snozzle—their iron grip on this place would loosen and their power base crumble.

You're in? Splendid! Splendid! We'll have to play our cards right, of course, we'll need to trust one another. I'll see if I can recruit some students to our cause.

Perhaps you can find one or two of your students to foment a little revolt? It shouldn't be too difficult to find some malcontents; then if things slide our way we can pop our little coup and have Thornblade, Crasston and Snozzle put down where they belong.

DAY TWO ~ *Ash Wednesday*

Chamber 101

Bell clanging. Crowd voices and movement. Slubgrip's voice is heard above the din.

Come to order! Come to order! Worms! Slimetoads! Grubs and Slugs, come to order!

This is Popular Culture 101. If you are meant to be in this class, then do me the courtesy of sitting down and shutting up. Now then, that's better. Nothing worse than starting off the day with your interminable grunting, squeaking and popping.

What's that? No, this is not Psychology and Psychosis taught by Dr. Froth. That's a third-level course—far above you. You may be confusing that course with Psychiatrists and Psychopaths. Professor Shrank teaches that next door. Off you go.

You are no doubt feeling gratified that you have not only moved up from paramecium, but progressed on to larva, and now you have graduated to the maggot class. However, remember that you are still worms, and you have an awful lot to learn, and much to suffer, before you can hope to move up to the next level. Remember fish bait, my dear fellows. Remember fish bait.

Grimwort you fat toad, do you have the attendance rosters ready? Well, get on with it—and stop sticking your tongue out like that. You know how it annoys me! Class, meet Grimwort, Associate Professor and my general dogsbody. Grimwort has been longing to be made a full professor for years, but he doesn't really have what it takes, do you, Grimwort?

Allow me to introduce myself. I am Professor Slubgrip and this is Popular Culture 101, or as it is sometimes called, "Pop Cult." As you have moved from the larva class, you will have no doubt mastered the simpler levels of temptation. Professor Crapulous will have taken you through the basic dimensions of rage and violence, while Dr. Strangle's sessions on lust and perversion will, no doubt, have tickled your disgusting adolescent imaginations. I hope you will remember Tepshank's classic lectures on sloth and despair, not forgetting Dr. Snout's lessons on gluttony, drunkenness and addictions.

All that is behind you now, my dear flukes. If you have got this far, then you have passed the exams and shown at least a basic understanding of the foundations of the art of tempting. Those of you who have been at all observant will see that our class begins on the day the Enemy calls "Ash Wednesday." "Ash Wednesday" they call it! I'll show the miserable creatures ashes—but not before they have some flames first....but there I'm getting off track again. Let me see...

Oh yes, this horrible day begins the season they call Lent. It's an annual remembrance of Our Father Below's encounter with that fraudulent carpenter from Nazareth. To counteract this hideous observance we will observe a six-week intensive course—meeting here every day Monday through Friday. On Saturday and Sunday I will hand you over to a series of guest lecturers who will instruct you in his or her own specialized area of expertise.

Be ready for some hard work, and be assured that I have your files on record. I know every moment of laziness, every betrayal—every failure. I know how each one of you miserable nematodes lost souls to the Enemy. I know the excuses you made. I know how you wriggled and squirmed and squeaked and screamed when it was your turn to be devoured at the banquet below. I know how you languished in the dark, frozen lands before your miserable parts were collected up and formed again first into paramecia and flatworms, then into a revolting, slimy larva. I know your whole sad and despicable histories, my dear worms, and believe me, I won't let you forget it.

Therefore, over the next few sessions, we will be considering the delightful area of temptation called popular culture, and Toad Grimwort and I shall have to crack the whip. Your minuscule brains will be stretched here, I can tell you, because we will be spending time on the background philosophies we have so carefully crafted which make our successes in the realm of popular culture so easy to maintain and cultivate.

Before you go, write down your homework assignment. I want you to start reading your textbook—chapter one, "Relativism and Reality"—in preparation for Friday's lecture. Class dismissed. Grimwort, look sharp. Hand out those homework schedules like I told you!

Footsteps. Student voices rise and rumble. Snoring is heard. A shriek of pain. Voice of Slubgrip:

Slurge—Get off Norman's back! No need to sink your teeth into him just because he dumped salt on your head. Learn to take a joke, dear boy. Learn to take a joke.

DAY THREE ~ *Thursday After Ash Wednesday*

Chamber 101

Door closes. Bell clanging. Crowd voices and movement. Voice of Slubgrip:

Grimwort, where is my prod? How am I to maintain discipline without my lightning bolt? Ahh, there it is. *(A sizzling sound then a yelp is heard.)* Hah!, now look lively old toad.

Listen up, slugs. Before we master chapter one in depth, we should stop to remember a few trenchant facts about your future clients. What you must never forget is that the humans are half-breeds. They are both physical and spiritual beings at the same time.

For some reason, the Enemy created a physical universe. Within this material world he made a complete range of beasts who snuffle around eating, breeding and generally being beastly. On the top of the heap are the apes who live together and pick fleas from one another. Some of these apes he has given eternal souls. Can you believe it? Our best minds still cannot figure out what the Enemy was thinking.

These half-ape, half-angels live in the physical world. You must remember that what seems to us to be nothing but a dark, viscous substance, like the stuff the mortals call molasses, is for them a bright, crisp and seemingly solid world of "reality." The repugnant beasts think this muddy mess called "the physical world" is delightful.

I am reminding you of this, my dear worms, because it is this physical realm that you will use to draw them down into our own delightful territory. Yes, yes, I hear you Slurge. Have the courtesy, if you will, to raise your emergent claw when you want to make a comment. It is true that their physicality is also the thing which can lift them up to the Enemy, but we must work around that.

What I want to focus on in this session, is the fact that they believe the physical realm to be "more real" than the spiritual realm. Most of your clients firmly believe that the only reality is what they can sense with their physical bodies. We have led them to believe that "seeing is believing." This is one of their basic assumptions. Consequently, what they cannot see they cannot believe in, and what they can see, they believe to be real, and by "real" they mean it really exists, that it is true, factual, solid and reliable. Of course you must never allow them to question the nature of perception and the fact that what they call "sight" is highly ambiguous. Keep it simple, worms. "Seeing is believing" is one of Our Father's most clever sound bytes. Use it.

This belief is very much to our advantage since we can then manipulate what they see and therefore what they believe in.

You there, you're Snort, aren't you? The slug next to you has fallen asleep. Bite him and wake him up, will you? Bite him hard. I want him to learn a lesson. *(A yelp is heard.)* Ahh. That's better. Welcome to the land of the living. What's your name? Shanklin? Fall asleep again, Shanklin, and I'll bite you myself, and not a little nip like Snort gave you, but I'll sink my fangs in you and take a chunk of your fat wormy flesh. Understand?

As I was saying, we control what they see and therefore what they believe. This is why, from the beginning we have been more interested in images than ideas. What they see is invariably linked with their desire. If they see something pretty, they want it for themselves.

Offer them baubles, my worms. Offer them trinkets and toys. Offer them anything that sparkles and sizzles and stimulates. Offer them action, explosions and entertainment. Keep them dazzled and delighted. Keep them amazed and marveling. From the moment they open their little peepers in the morning until their eyelids droop at night, give them something—almost anything—to look at.

Start by keeping them distracted from the Enemy and soon distraction will lead to deception.

Tomorrow I will be lecturing on "Relativism and Reality." Remember on Saturdays and Sundays there will be special guest lecturers. Did you think you would have time off on the weekends? Not likely. We must keep at it, worms. Remember, there's no rest for the dreary.

A bell clangs.

Class dismissed.

DAY FOUR ~ *Friday After Ash Wednesday*

Chamber 101

The groaning and grinding of distant machinery. Door closes. Crowd voices and movement. A bell is clanging. Voice of Slubgrip:

Come to order, slugs. Grimwort, nip down to the lounge and get me a cup of lava, will you? You know what I like best—fresh ground pusher with a dash of meth, and bring me a couple of tablets. I've got a splitting headache.

Now then worms, today I wish to share with you one of Our Father Below's greatest accomplishments. It is a work of pure genius. A most delightful bit of sleight of hand called "relativism." Relativism simply means that there is no such thing as truth. Once Our Father Below realized that anything might be good or evil depending on the circumstances or intentions, the rest was a piece of cake.

I know it is hard to grasp, but try to remember that the humans are half-ape and half-angel. They have beastly physical bodies, they also have spirits. They aspire for higher things. They long to be perfect. The problem is, their physical natures are at war with their spiritual natures. Are you still with me, worms?

We hear a door opening. Footsteps.

Grimwort, you incompetent fool! I asked for a dash of meth in my lava, and you bring me this disgusting cup of ordinary sewage? Where's my prod? *(A sizzling sound, then yelp from Grimwort.)* Perhaps that will teach you to be more careful, you fat toad.

Now concentrate if you can, worms. The Enemy tries to get around this clash between their spiritual and physical sides by forgiving them when they slip back into ape-like behaviors. Why he does so is beyond me. He's soft, that's why. What they deserve is punishment, but he lets them off the hook. There's nothing I'd like better than getting them on the hook—the meat hook.

What you must do with your patients is show them that the ideal behaviors are unrealistic. Remind them of the Enemy's ten commandments, and help them see that they are simply impossible. "Thou shalt not lie"? What, never? "If a man looks on a woman with lust in his heart he has committed adultery?" Surely not. You see? The standards he sets for the little cretins are far too high. Whisper in their ears that they are attempting the impossible. The goals of perfection that their spiritual side demands are incompatible with the physical world they live in.

Don't make them *think* that all things are relative. Get them to *feel* that all things are relative. One of the best ways to do this is to use hypothetical situations. Come up with a particularly juicy, wicked action, then engage them in a game in which they invent a situation and intention that would make that action good. (Our philosophy department has come up with a whole industry along these lines called "situation ethics.")

Let's say your patient believes that killing an unborn child is wrong. Get him to see that the child would be born into a dysfunctional family, have a terrible life and be condemned to a life of misery. Get him to see that the mother would ruin her career and be condemned to a life of poverty herself. He must see that he is not killing an unborn child; he is helping the poor woman in a crisis pregnancy. Let him hear someone shouting, "Every child should be a wanted child!"

You see how it goes. Virtually every moral choice can be made relative in this way, and once the moral choices are made relative, it is an easy matter for religious dogma to be similarly neutralized. Before long he will agree with you that there is no such thing as religious truth, just as he has already concluded that there is no such thing as moral truth. Hammer it home, worms. Weave this into everything you do.

The results will be very pleasing. The multitudes of indifferent humans who end up in our banqueting house below may not be very tasty or succulent victims, but we must have staples as well as delicacies. They may be bland, but we can grind their bones to make our bread.

Tomorrow my old friend Zelnick will be your guest lecturer. He's a major player in the film industry. Starlow will be here on Sunday. She's quite the old warhorse. I think you'll be entertained.

Class dismissed. I say there, Snort. Stay behind for a moment, will you? I've got a few things I'd like to discuss with you...

DAY FIVE ~ *Saturday After Ash Wednesday*

Chamber 101

Door closes. Bell clanging. Crowd voices and movement. A gruff, smoky voice is heard. It is the demon Zelnick:

Slubgrip told me you guys were a pain in the behind. Now sit down, will you? Listen, I got connections. OK? You don't want to sit there and pay attention, I can call the Flancks right now. Grimwort, hand me that prod. I need to light my cigar.

I guess Slubgrip was telling you about that "seeing is believing" line? It's a good one. So the old boy tells me he's talking to you about philosophy. My opinion is too much of that stuff is risky. If they start thinking things through, you never know where it's going to lead. Philosophy? Fugeddaboudit. Keep them dazzled and they'll never have time to think things through.

For centuries all we had was the theatrical stage. What a huge pain in the behind it all was with pulleys and props and prima donnas—all that trooping about and la-di-da stuff! All the time you have to put up with these so-called stars. The main point is that through the theater we were able to give the mongrels something to entertain and amuse them. They identified with what they saw (remember "seeing is believing"); and by tempting the playwrights and producers to cater to the lowest taste of the audience, we were able to sway the minds of the brutes simply by spinning a good yarn in an entertaining way.

I don't mind telling you there was a risk. The Enemy is cunning and he's cheap. He don't mind stealing our best ideas and flipping them for his purposes. Me and my boys were doing a good job with that treacherous, atheist playwright Christopher Marlowe and then what do you know? The Enemy allows Marlowe to get bumped off and he comes up with William Shakespeare.

Geesh, what's that smell? Who was that? Shanklin? I'm not surprised.

Slubgrip said you were a stinker. Snort, tell you what, why don't you sit back there next to Shanklin. If he drops another stink bug or if he falls asleep, you know what to do. You weren't given fangs for decoration.

Now, where was I? Oh yeah, "Seeing is believing." First they invented photography, then motion pictures and then the computer screen. Now we are at the point where the humans are entering "the age of the screen." The chimps with souls now spend huge amounts of their time staring at a screen. Television screens, movie screens, iPads, smart phones, animated billboards, smart boards in schools...the list goes on. They play games on the screen, talk with each other on the screen, watch movies on the screen, do homework on the screen, do office work on the screen, watch news on the screen. I Screen. You Screen! We all Screen for iScreen!!

This is a success for us. Big time.

Not only do we control most of what they see on these screens, but best of all, it takes the miserable vermin out of what the Enemy calls "ordinary reality." Instead of that we give them a reality of our own making. Listen, kids, if you do your job right in this industry, you can use the screens to lure them into some very good stuff: Lust, Envy, Rage, Murder, Witchcraft, Necromancy, Pride, Sloth, Gluttony. It's easy. They love to watch flickering, entrancing images, and I mean "entrancing." We want them to be hypnotized, enchanted and charmed. We want them to fall under our spell.

The thing is, you can't let down your guard. You know what I mean? The Enemy will use the screens as well. Before you know it they'll be watching a film into which one of his lackeys has slipped a "redemptive theme." Those kind of preachy movies make me sick. You want to send a message? Send a telegram! The other lousy thing is that even our best workers—the film makers who are in it to get rich—realize that a "good story" sells and that the hairless brutes go all sentimental and insist that the "good guys" win while our own characters are defeated.

Anyhow, tomorrow Starlow is going to give you a talk about show business. She's an old trooper. You'll like her.

DAY SIX ~ *Sunday,* First Week of Lent

Chamber 101

Door closes. Bell clanging. Crowd voices and movement. Some whistles, murmurs and catcalls. A low, lush and fruity female voice is heard. It is the demon Starlow:

Thank you, boys. Thank you. Imagine dear Slubgrip inviting an old has-been like me to lecture his class! Why, I never thought in a million years I'd be so honored! What a good-looking class of slugs! Here's lookin' at you, boys!

More whistles and catcalls...

You're too good to me. You know I used to be as white as snow...but I drifted.

Roars of approval and howling laughter.

That's right...*sings...* "there's no business like show business!" That's our theme today, flukes. Yes, today we want to talk about show business... *she sings...* "The minute he walks through the door..."

More whistles and catcalls...

Thank you, boys. I suppose even a washed-up old starlet like me still has a bit of the old sparkle, eh? A bit of the old razzmatazz?
Let's get serious, boys. I did a bit of the old va-va-voom to remind you that the poor hairless nincompoops go all goggle-eyed with a little bit of razzle dazzle—a dash of smoke and mirrors here, a flash of sequins and a feather boa there. Here a little wiggle—there a bat of the eye...a little nudge...a little wink?

That's entertainment, and it's entertainment we use to cast a spell. We keep them titillated and diverted with entertainment—so much so that anything the Enemy presents will then seem hopelessly dull.

You see, boys, if we get them hooked on entertainment it isn't long before anything that requires concentration or hard work will be boring. That's why we have to constantly raise the entertainment dosage. This is because what we are offering them—we must admit it, dear boys—is sometimes a little bit shallow. The maddening thing is that the Enemy actually wants the brutes to enjoy themselves.

He's devised this horrible idea of leisure. Makes me froth at the mouth! Furthermore, he has planted in their hearts the longing for eternal leisure. I can't think of anything worse, to tell you the honest truth. What, are they supposed to sit around all day long doing nothing at all? Are they to sip tea and chat with one another while endless ages run? What do they do the whole time? Do they play volleyball or pinochle? Do they frolic in the sea or sit on rocking chairs on the porch and play checkers world without end, Amen? It's disgusting.

I'm getting off track. Here is my point: I'm happy to say that those very clever fellows down below have taken this revolting idea called "leisure" and turned it into something far more pleasing, which we call entertainment!

The half-breeds now expect to be entertained constantly. And it's your job to keep them hooked. I know for you it is all rather dreary. Not everyone can enjoy the smell of the greasepaint, the roar of the crowd!

You'll have to sit with your patient while he channel-hops until he is so bored that he will even watch re-runs of *Gilligan's Island* or *I Dream of Jeannie* or programs about home makeovers.

The most delightful consequence of cultivating their addiction to entertainment is that they have now turned worship into entertainment. They have what they call "mega churches" with huge screens, rock music, dry ice, dancers and "relevant" preachers who hypnotize their audience with inspiring stories, captivating methods of communication and a reassuringly shallow message of self-help, sentimentality and "spirituality"--whatever that is. Happily there is little mention of that grubby little loser from Nazareth.The exciting truth is that the brutes now expect their churches to be as entertaining as a Las Vegas floor show.

Just keep them entertained. Keep them hypnotized with any form of entertainment until they finally come to believe that all there is in life is entertainment.

If a bit of reality or suffering jolts them awake, they'll be so disappointed and angry that with just a teeny little push they will tumble over into a nice pit of despair, and with another nudge you'll have them wallowing nicely in a soup of self-pity, cynicism and rage.

A bell clangs.

Hell's bells! Is that the time? Toodle loo, dear boys. I've got to run! This little baby's got to see a fellow about a really big deal. He says he's making a picture and I'm the one! Imagine, little old me up there on the silver screen!

DAY SEVEN ~ *Monday,* First Week of Lent

Chamber 101

Bell clanging. Door slams. Crowd voices and movement. Slubgrip:

Grimwort, I rely on you to get these slime worms in line. Instead, I arrive a few minutes late, only to find them slouching, squelching and oozing in a disgusting manner. If you can't be a bit sharper and wield the fork with a bit of finesse I'll find another associate.

Now then, nematodes. I'm going to stretch those poor brains of yours with a touch of philosophy. I know it is a yawn for you, but if you don't do the foundations, you'll never understand the filigree.

Last week I explained relativism. Everything else we do is built on it, and we couldn't get this first lie across without the help of what the mortals call "higher education." You may think our great successes are in the brothels, beer halls and betting shops, but all of that is small change compared to the triumphs we have achieved in the exalted heights of academe—the quads and squares of Oxbridge and the ivory towers of the Ivy League.

The fact of the matter is, we won control of their higher education long ago, and with this, everything else in their popular culture has tumbled like dominoes. You would have thought that higher education couldn't stand up if there were no such thing as truth. You might say, "no truth, no learning," but we've side-stepped that little difficulty and turned relativism into a virtual industry. You see, once there is no truth, there is an enormous amount of academic-type work to be done constantly dismantling all the "truth" that's out there and discussing what "might be true in a particular situation."

The truth of the matter is that it is not easy keeping the relativism show on the road. This ludicrous "truth" thing keeps popping up its ugly head. In addition to our work in the universities we attack the concept of "truth" from every angle. We do this through a multitude of philosophic sub-categories which we will consider in the rest of this course.

What's that, Slurge? Yes, I did use the word "truth" a moment ago; however, what I *meant* by it was only metaphorical. I used the word "truth" as if it might in some metaphorical sense have "meaning." I was not implying that there is any such thing as objective truth. You and I know that there is no such thing, and therefore my use of the word, was only, as it were, a turn of phrase.

How dare you come up with that idiotic argument, saying, "But if there's no such thing as truth, how do we know that the statement 'there's no such thing as truth' is true?" Slurge, I thought you were cleverer than that. That question is simply a case of semantics. You're playing with words and abstract concepts that have no meaning. It's sophomoric mumbo jumbo and I won't dignify it with a response.

Let's get back to the point. Remember, worms, relativism begins with moral relativism and moves to philosophical relativism. Get them to compromise their morals and before long they will compromise everything.

During the rest of the course we'll discuss how to weave relativism into practically everything you touch in popular culture. It's a fine art, my dear flukes and annelids. Master it, and you may pass the exams and move up to the crustacean class. Why, one day you may even ascend to the heights of master like me, your dear professor. There's the bell. Class dismissed.

Noise of gruntings, shoving and snorting as the students leave the class. Slubgrip calls above the rumble of the rabble:

I say Snort, have you remembered our meeting tomorrow?

DAY EIGHT ~ *Tuesday,* First Week of Lent

The Lavatory Coffee Shoppe

Sounds of burping and gurgling lava percolating.

Ahh, Snort! Good of you to take a few moments to join me for a cup of lava. How do you like yours? A splash of society lush with a sprinkle of chocolate addict, or do you take your lava like you take your demonettes— hot, red and barefoot?

What about a piece of cake? There's a pretty prostitute cupcake here with lust icing— or what about this devil's food cake? Mouthwatering.

I expect you're wondering why I've asked you here. The fact of the matter is, I've got a proposal for you. It is obvious to me that you are the top of your class. That is why I have asked you to be class monster—I mean monitor. How you were ever flushed down to the lower levels in the first place is beyond me. I can't imagine that you ever put a foot wrong in this skillful war of temptation!

I can see that you're not only streaks ahead of your fellow slugs, but that you will not be with us very long. No doubt the Administration will soon hear about your brilliance and President Thornblade will bump you up to the amphibians in no time. After that you'll clear reptile class and be back to dragon and full-blown demon.

You may be wondering what this little talk is all about, so let me come straight to the point. It has been brought to my attention that there has been some very unpleasant gossip about me in the upper levels of the faculty. You know how it is with gossip. One little misunderstanding and before you know it, people have got the wrong end of the stick and stories start swirling. I understand people are talking about an occurrence in my past.

I expect you have heard the rumors, too? Some centuries ago, one of my patients was a young Spaniard named Ignatius who became a missionary. It is true that he slipped through my claws and went on to accomplish great things for the Enemy, but I assure you that it was not my fault, and the stories of my complacency and failure are greatly exaggerated.

These unfortunate rumors are hindering my own advancement, and although I dearly love teaching Popular Culture 101 to you and your charming young colleagues, it is clear that I have another destiny. I suppose you know Commissioner Crasston and Dr. Snozzle? They're old friends of mine who are now in charge of Security and Detention.

Well, now Snort, there's the crux of the matter (if you'll excuse the expression)—it seems that Crasston and Snozzle have bought into the lies that are being spread about me and have me down for a thoroughly disloyal demon, and one who should be relegated and not advanced. It would do me a world of good if we had a certain amount of (shall we say) "success" in the Popular Culture classroom.

You know one of the unpleasant things about working here below is that there is a constant atmosphere of plotting, back-stabbing and character assassination. It's a dreadful truth that you simply cannot trust anyone these days. You think someone is a loyal friend and an amiable colleague only to find that he has been betraying you to security, lying about you to friends and planning bitter revenge. It really can be most tiresome.

Consequently, there is always some sort of rebellion or other brewing: here a student protest, there a faculty strike. So here's my idea: There's nothing Our Father Below likes better than to have rebellion in the ranks dealt with quite severely. I thought you might like to stir up a bit of discontent among the other students—not for real of course—just a bit of fun. Then, if I were seen to be putting down this little "rebellion" ruthlessly, my own stock would go up with Crasston and Snozzle. Of course, once my own advancement to the next level were assured, I would not forget you, dear boy. I'm sure your own speedy promotion would soon follow.

There's something further in it for you too, Snort. If you happen to have one or two enemies—and who doesn't? You can draw them into the game. Put them out front as the leaders of the revolt. Then when I call in the Flancks they'll be the first to be rounded up and sent below to the chokey.

You might start with Shanklin. He's a particularly callow slug, not very bright or committed. I will continue to make him the butt of my ridicule and put him down every chance I get. Why don't you see if you can get next to him, encourage his bitterness and bile? Gather a few others and make them think President Thornblade is to blame for their problems. You should stay in the background. When the Flancks descend, we don't want you to be caught in their net.

You're in? Marvelous! Marvelous! We'll keep it all secret, of course, now won't we?

DAY NINE ~ *Wednesday,* First Week of Lent

Chamber 101

Door closes. Bell clanging. Crowd voices and movement. Slubgrip:

Grimwort, prod those late comers, will you?*(A yelp.)* That's better. Move along slugs, move along.

I hope you have read the next chapter of your text—"Individualism and Anarchy." Now pay attention as I outline the various forms of relativism that we cultivate in popular culture.

Shanklin, do stop sniveling there like a seventh-grade human female. It's a disgusting habit. So you've been bullied a bit. So what? It should toughen you up, but all you do is cry like a baby maggot. In my experience those who are bullied usually deserve it. Move to the back of the class at once. I can't bear to be near you. That's right, sit next to Snort. Perhaps he'll be a good influence on you.

My dear worms, one of the main ways of making relativism stick is to ensure that your patient considers himself to be the center of the universe. I'm talking about individualism. This is the idea that each individual is the sole arbiter not only of taste, but of moral choices, political ideas, religious beliefs—everything.

You must nurture in your patient the idea that he is unique. If he has any form of artistic talent, make him believe that he is one of a kind—a solitary, unappreciated genius. "The lonely poet starving in his garrett"— that sort of thing. If your patient is more inclined to business or sports, build up an image in his mind of the lone figure at the top of his profession. Give him an image of himself as a titan among mere mortals.

That's like you, isn't it, Grimwort? The lonely talented genius? The unappreciated magnificent Master Tempter Toad? Master of the Mediocre, I'd say.

Laughter, snorts, howls and giggles.

This individualism I'm talking about has many side benefits, worms. First of all, a nice crop of pride can be grown in the little brute's soul. Secondly...are you taking notes?...you can get your patient to imagine that because of his genius he is above the law. Is there a pesky moral regulation keeping him back? Tell him he is above those petty rules. He is one of the great ones. Thirdly, use his individualism to keep him isolated from ordinary people with common sense—he will especially avoid the types who might pop his balloon and tell him what an arrogant imbecile he is. Fourthly, it is easy to lead certain types from individualism into eccentricity and then from eccentricity into perversion and from perversion into downright depravity. I once had a patient who was so proud of being "different" that he explored ever more depraved pleasures and ended up abducting and torturing small children. Ahh, those were the days!

What we want for most of our patients is for each to assume that they are the ones who make all the choices. They decide everything. It goes without saying that they must reject any form of authority or external discipline.

One of my favorite lines to use in this respect is "Judge not that ye be not judged." Get your patient to memorize this one, and when anyone should dare to correct them, or suggest that there is a right and wrong way to behave, you can get them to shriek, "Who do you think you are to judge me!!"

Of course, like all these things, it cuts both ways. While you want to encourage this sort of individualism, you want to watch that you don't take it too far. We want our patients to assert their individualism, but we certainly do not want them to do anything courageously individualistic in the service of the Enemy.

Snoot was developing a girl into an individualistic, lonely artist type. She had cut herself off from all her "normal" friends and started to be reclusive. She could have been formed into a pleasing eccentric who went down the path of weirdness and depravity, but Snoot allowed the girl to start reading about that nauseating French girl Thérèse Martin, and before long the Enemy agents pulled a reversal and the girl ended up becoming a missionary sister working in a slum. This is just the sort of devious trick the Enemy likes to pull. You spend so long developing a patient along a certain path, and he uses the very thing you were working on to pull the rug out from under you.

Individualism is the best way to turn your patient into an arrogant, ignorant self-righteous egotist. Keep him sated in his overwhelming self-regard, but as soon as he starts thinking that he might do something brave, noble and excellent which would make him stand out from the crowd, remind him that he doesn't want to be thought of as an oddball, a snob or someone who is "weird."

There's the bell. Off you go, slugs. Read chapter three for tomorrow on eclecticism.

DAY TEN ~ *Thursday,* First Week of Lent

Chamber 101

Shuffling sounds. Furniture shifting. Low mumbles and rumbles of voices. Slubgrip:

Eclecticism is a long word, slugs, but write it down. It's not that difficult a concept to grasp. Even you, Shanklin, may finally absorb some knowledge if you apply yourself.

To be eclectic is to gather up random things or ideas of interest—like grandma's attic or one of those odd museums with bibelots, oddities and curiosities from one's travels.

Look at it like this: your patient sees that the modern world is increasingly multicultural. In any town you see restaurants from around the world. You see individuals from Africa, Asia, Europe and America all living together. You hear different languages and see different customs.

The same is true of religions. Where there was once only Christianity in their culture, now you have Islam, Buddhism, Mormonism and a thousand other beliefs. It is much easier, therefore, to get your human to think that all religions are the same. Get them to think of religions as they do restaurants. There is an Indian restaurant and an Italian restaurant and a Chinese restaurant. Likewise there is Hinduism, Catholicism, Buddhism. You check the menu and you make your choice. Whisper in your human's ear that all the religions are the same and choosing a religion is only a matter of taste.

The idea that all religions are the same is called indifferentism. Indifferentism is the lazy sister of syncretism. Syncretism is the active embrace of all religions. Eclecticism is similar to syncretism, except the patient who is being eclectic picks parts of different religions like being in a religious buffet. Are you taking notes?

Grimwort! Despicable toad! Have you fallen asleep when you were supposed to be monitoring student behavior? Give me my fork.

A yelp is heard from Grimwort.

That's right. Not a fork in the road, but a fork in the toad.

Laughter, howls, grunts and giggles.

I once had a patient who was a moderately intelligent college student. He became interested in Scientology because a movie star he admired was a devotee. He added to this a belief in reincarnation because he'd read a story on the internet about an Englishwoman who claimed to be a reincarnated Egyptian princess. He mixed in some positive thinking ideas from a few self-help books; his beliefs on personal morality were taken from a blog run by an anarchist group; and he believed in the paranormal as a result of a combination of horror films, violent video games and a book on exorcism that his Catholic grandmother lent him. He believed Jesus Christ was a "pretty cool teacher" as a result of one week in Vacation Bible School when he was ten, and he sometimes went to a local Evangelical church with a girlfriend where he once "accepted Jesus Christ as his personal Lord and Savior" because the girl thought it would be good if he did.

That's what I mean by eclecticism. Part of the charm of eclecticism is to make sure your patient considers all religions to be man-made.

Once he sees that they are man-made, he'll draw the conclusion that there's no need to practice a particular religion. He'll soon affirm with glowing pride that he is "spiritual but not religious." This brilliant invention of our best educationalists means that the hairless chimp will, on the one hand, believe himself to be spiritually superior to all those "dull people who have to go to church every week" while at the same time he will make absolutely zero progress toward the land of the Enemy.

A bell clangs.

DAY ELEVEN ~ *Friday,* First Week of Lent

Chamber 101

There is an dull rumble of argument. A voice is heard saying, "I'd like to see that Crasston and Snozzle get a taste of their own medicine." *Another says,* "What about old Thornblade? You can't trust him, you know…"

Slubgrip's voice rises above the others:

What's all this? I couldn't help overhearing. Do I discern a touch of rebellion in the ranks? A good old-fashioned student protest is brewing? I hope not. Believe me, dear fellows, the Flancks will have no mercy. The smallest act of rebellion will be rooted out and you will find yourselves with an invitation to dinner. Don't spit on the Master, my friends, or you'll soon find yourself on the Master's spit.

Now let's get started. Sentimentalism is our subject today.

Grimwort, old toad, bring me my tablets and a glass of fumes, will you? It's my head. It feels like it's in a vise that's slowly being tightened…

Where was I? Oh yes, the hairless bipeds like to think that they are rational creatures. Happily, very few of them decide anything at all on a rational basis. They decide not by what they think, but how they feel. Their emotions drive most of their decisions, and those decisions not driven by their emotions are driven by their groins.

Confuse them, fiends. We don't want them to be rational, and we use popular culture to dull their rational faculties. Allowing them to think too much is a risky business. Much better to keep them operating on the emotional or hormonal level.

Pay attention, slugs. This is important! There are three levels of emotion. The brute level we call "instinct." This is the level at which the brutes breed, fight, feed and feel rage or joy. The next level of emotion we call "sentiment." At this level their emotions have been educated somewhat. They have learned higher emotions like patriotism, love of family, a concern for justice or fair play, reverence for older people and kindness towards children. The highest level we call "passion." This is when their brute emotions are linked to some great cause.

We want to avoid passion altogether. Emotion is good. You should keep them on the brutish, instinctual level, but they usually feel ashamed and disgusted with themselves at that level. Sentimentality is best. They like that. It makes them feel all warm and uplifted about themselves.

The images we produce to make them sentimentalists should pull on their heartstrings. Use puppy dogs, kittens, little children and grandparents to make them feel warm and sweet. Use soldiers, flags, coffins and grand landscapes to make them feel patriotic and brave. Use home, hearth and happy teenagers, youthful mothers and handsome fathers to make them feel the glow of nostalgia. Make sure the warm and lovely sentiments do not lead them to any positive action. Keep the sentimentality flowing through the images. Keep it light and fluffy and keep it constant.

Grimwort, I see you muttering. You think sentimentality is beneath you, but you don't realize the subtlety of it. You see, worms, as the brutes stopped believing in any such thing as "truth," they subsequently stopped believing in any such thing as virtue. Having done so, all they have left is sentimentality, and this is what we can now manipulate with great skill through popular culture.

If you are successful, your patient will soon be in a sweetly hypnotized state in which he is so swamped with sweet images that he will think "niceness" is the only virtue. "Niceness" will soon translate into "tolerance" so that anyone who tolerates them will be considered "nice" and those who do not will be thought "not nice."

Grimwort doesn't believe me, but in this state of mind—sated with sentimentality—you can lure your patient into every kind of intemperance, sexual promiscuity and selfish pleasure. All you need to do is show him other "nice" people doing these things. Before long he will be addicted to his new habits, and anyone who opposes them will be seen as "intolerant," "not nice" or "not normal," and these "not nice" people will not only seem a threat; they will seem like the enemy.

From there, with just a little push your patient will quite happily wish for such intolerant people to be arrested, fined or even imprisoned, and he will do so all the time believing himself to be ridding the world of intolerant people who are "not nice." One of the most delightful results of pushing sentimentality is to see someone bully and manipulate others by being "nice."

One of my patients bullied an entire school into hiring a monster of a teacher simply because the person was a member of a racial minority and my patient felt sorry for him and bullied everyone by blackmailing them emotionally. She tried to make everyone else else feel sorry for him, too. The monster of a teacher was horrible to children and incompetent, and finally ruined the school. No one dared to get rid of him because of sentimentality.

Read the next chapter on hedonism for Monday, and remember on Saturdays and Sundays you have guest speakers. Tomorrow my old friend Karmeleon will be here to give his very interesting views on spiritual growth, and on Sunday Swagger will speak on the uses of sentimentality in religion.

Time's up, worms. Get to work. Remember your failures. Remember why you were returned to the maggotry. Remember the motto of Our Father Below: "Eat or be eaten".

A bell clangs.

DAY TWELVE ~ *Saturday*, First Week of Lent

Chamber 101

The sound of raucous screeching and slurping. Bites and yelps. Furniture being thrown. Someone screams, "Down with the detention!" Another, "Crasston means corruption!" There is a sound of glass shattering...

A calm, mellow voice is heard.

Friends. I will remain in silence until you join me.

Screams of terror and sounds of mayhem. Cursing and howling. Eventually one deep voice dominates. It is Associate Professor Grimwort.

If you slugs don't calm down, you know what will happen! The listening devices will pick up this rebellion and the Flancks will be here in no time. Then we'll all be in the soup. Literally.

Now calm down and listen to the professor here. It's Karmeleon, the famous spiritual guru.

The mayhem quietens down, and the mellow voice is heard again.

Thank you, my friend. Thank you. Violence, my friends, is the last resort of the incompetent. All things may be reconciled with quiet conversation. Listen to one another. Dialogue. Yes. Listen more than you speak.

My dear friend and old colleague Professor Slubgrip has asked me to speak to you today about the influence of spirituality in popular culture.

Dear students. Think for a moment about the need which the sad and narrow-minded humans have for something called "doctrine." This is a discursive statement of a spiritual principle they wish to call "truth." However, we will not fall into that trap. Instead of a statement of "truth" which is supposed to be an answer, we wish to propose a question. Notice that we do not impose. We propose. We propose a question rather than impose an answer.

The question is this: "How can something as expansive and mysterious as the concept they call 'God' be contained in a formulation of words? How can God be contained in something as manufactured as a religion, a sacred book, a creed or a dogma?" When this most basic question is posed, it is not long before the religious client is drawn away from what is called "organized religion" into what we call "spirituality."

Help your patient to see that organized religion is a prison house. Once he is free from the constraints of religion, he will most certainly be yours completely. Then he can be taken in a number of different directions.

Most of those you liberate from religion to spirituality will use their new freedom to indulge in all their own selfish desires. They will call their sexual promiscuity "sexual liberation." They will call their new addictions "liberating experiences" and their complete abandonment of all morality "self-expression." Indeed, with a bit of ingenuity you may get them to believe that their "liberating experiences" are part of their spiritual awakening. I once had a patient who was very nicely addicted to drugs because he thought they brought him closer to God.

With some application, patience and skill you may take your patient from the simple level of "spiritual but not religious" to a far more subtle and long-lasting expression of this state of mind. To do this you must encourage your patient to explore alternative spiritualities.

Let them have a "spiritual experience" of some sort. They will be so thrilled that they will do most anything to repeat their glimpse into our side of reality. The spiritual experience will have the added benefit of convincing them that they are spiritually superior. I do not need to emphasize how pleasing this is.

From their spiritual experiences they can be drawn into the hidden arts of spirituality, which was once called "the occult." Start with a fascination with astrology, ecology and earth powers. It's only a short move from there to neo-paganism, fortune telling, and necromancy. Along with these many side attractions you will wish to introduce them to the practice called "channeling." In this delightful tradition they actually open their minds and souls to become channels of "creative life forces"— which is another term for ourselves, dear friends.

There is a snarl, growl, snap and the crash of glass. Suddenly a yelp. Grimwort's voice is heard:

You there, Morgan and Frack. Settle down or I'll use the prod again! Snort, give me the fork, will you?

DAY THIRTEEN ~ *Sunday,* Second Week of Lent

Chamber 101

Sounds of squirming, squelching and squealing. A door slams.

Sit down, boys. Swagger's here!

Murmuring of anticipation and glee. Sliding of seats and sudden quiet.

Slubgrip called me in to teach you all a little bit about the ole-time religion. I'm talking the sawdust trail, the revival tent, the TV ministry and the radio Bible hour. What we're talking about is a sweet little false religion.

It's a pretty good game if you can get it. You see the sad lonely humans are just as desperate as can be for a religion that feeds them sweetness and light and makes them feel all good about themselves. First thing you need is a decent preacher. It don't matter if he's Protestant or Catholic. Shucks, it don't matter if he's Pentecostal or Episcopal. Hell's bells! It don't even matter if he's Mormon or Muslim. The main thing is he's gotta be a good preacher. He needs to know how to get 'em all stirred up and emotional. That's the thing. Emotion.

This is all part of this relativism stuff you've been working on with ole Slubgrip. I'm talking about the idea that there's no true religion. Make them remember that all religion is man-made.

So first you get yourself a good preacher. You gotta work on him first, boys. Get him to think it's all about him and the love he's getting from his people. Butter him up. Make sure he gets good reviews and let his church start growing. Don't forget the money! When he starts talking about "evangelizing" and "church growth" you make sure he starts seeing dollar signs. He says "saving souls" but he means "savings account." If he's a smart cookie he'll soon figure out what brings folks through the door and what drives them away, and he'll soon learn how to deliver.

That's when you start working on the folks in the pews. Work together as a team, fellas! Get the people in the pews to call the shots. We don't want no preachers telling them about hell and damnation and sin and repentance. No sirree! You get that preacher to tell them about love and peace and forgiveness and healing. Get him to tell them stories about little children and brave soldiers and grandma who used to pray on her knees every night 'til she wore out the floorboards.

Before too long you have a mutual admiration society between the preacher and his people. Like I say, it don't matter if he's a Protestant or a Catholic. It works both ways. What happens is the preacher never says nothing to upset his fan club, and the fan club continues to dish out the love he needs—not to mention the cash! You get a religion rolling along like that and you're coming out on top! You're going to find yourself demon of the year!

Why, it just tickles me pink to think of a whole boatload of souls drifting down to Our Father Below, all the while thinking that they're just the most wonderful Christian people who ever walked this earth.

I tell you boys, if you get called into religion, it's one of the most fun places to play in the whole wide world! On the other hand, if you get stuck with some pastor or priest who knows his stuff and realizes that there's a spiritual battle on hand—why you've pulled the short straw, son.

Y'all better scoot. That bell went long ago, and if I keep you too long I know what'll happen—I'll get called up to Commissioner Crasston—and that ain't going to be no picnic.

DAY FOURTEEN ~ *Monday,* Second Week of Lent

Slubgrip's Lair

Slubgrip's voice:

Knobswart, you old reptile! Wonderful the way you've been able to turn your tutorial group into a little cell of revolutionaries! Your note last week about how you suggested that Thornblade, Crasston and Snozzle were a "Gang of Three" was truly inspired.

I also have some good news to report. My boy Snort has been doing a fine job stirring up discontent among the students. Last weekend Karmeleon took my class and found them most unruly. Snort has been especially keen to get a rather unpleasant and oafish student named Shanklin to lead the revolt.

Snort's also started a student newspaper called *Red*. Calling for democracy, equal votes for all levels of demons and weekends off. If he can raise some more of the rabble we should have a nice little revolt on our hands. I thought they might get a petition together as well, and this is how we might increase the pressure by getting the rest of the faculty on our side.

With that in mind, I'm having a little get-together at my place on Thursday night. I've invited the usual suspects, but do you think you could rouse a few more? I know most of the faculty are in fear of Thornblade, but if we simply bill it as a drinks party, do you think they might come along?

I think the way forward, Knobby, is for you to take the lead. You're so awfully good at speech-making and the rest of the faculty trusts you in a way they don't me. Perhaps you could begin by praising Thornblade, Crasston and Snozzle. I'll watch their reactions. There are bound to be a good number already fed up with the regime. When I give you the nod you might just move the speech in the right direction. I'm sure you'll think of something. Question whether Thornblade is really up to the job, point out Crasston and Snozzle's rather draconian regulations, all the paperwork they demand, the listening monitors, the demerit system and the constant threat of the Flancks, the Chokey and the Dark Hole.

Allow me to play the good cop. You take the speech against the regime just as far as you think you can, and then I'll step in and butter them up, saying it's not really as bad as all that. I'll suggest that it would be perfectly reasonable for faculty members to put together some sort of consultation committee that will liaise with the administration in order to enhance communications. You know the sort of thing. That will keep them feeling both dangerous and safe at the same time.

You think it's a brilliant plan? Do you really think so? Why Knobby, how very kind of you to say so! I think it will work as long as we are careful and play our cards right. Well, I must say, I haven't got where I am today by trusting others! You know what the master says, "Be wise as a serpent..."

Let's get the faculty together on Thursday, and in the meantime, I've been making friends with Crasston's secretary—a hot little demon named Flaunt. Over a glass of red and some fried gambler chips she confided in me. Did you know that Crasston has a secret file on Thornblade himself? He's keeping it until just the right moment in order to bring Thornblade down and step into the presidency. I'll see if I can get the file from Flaunt. This could fit into our plan very nicely. Depending on what's in the file, we could bring Thornblade down ourselves or else blow the whistle on Crasston.

Here's the name of Snozzle's right-hand man in Detention. Do you think you might ingratiate yourself with him, Knobby? You know, take him a little something? He's a corpulent old demon named Jabulon. Everybody calls him Jumbo. I understand he's a terribly crafty old goat, but that he's got a sweet tooth. Thought you might like to take him this lovely little fruitcake of perverts. Shall I wrap it up as a present? Here, take this bottle of sweet hypocrite too. It will complement the fruitcake nicely.

DAY FIFTEEN ~ *Tuesday,* Second Week of Lent

Chamber 101

Slubgrip's voice:

Come to attention, worms. I hope you have done your homework and read the chapter on hedonism. No, Crampton, not "heathenism," although it's not a bad comparison, I suppose.

Hedonism is the love of pleasure. To use a phrase coined by Our Father Below, "If it feels good, do it." This principle may seem obvious, and at a rather simplistic level it is the most basic form of temptation. However, this course is not simply a matter of teaching you the beginner's tricks. I'm trying to get you to think things through, and this pleasure business is rather more complex than simply getting your patient to gorge himself, get drunk and fornicate.

You need to see how the pleasure principle is woven into every aspect of popular culture. In one way or another, every form of entertainment, news item, book or television show revolves around the human's need for pleasure. Don't fall into the trap of imagining that our only goal is to get them to indulge in pleasure for its own sake. We want them not simply to indulge in pleasure, but to do so on our terms. Otherwise, their very desire for pleasure may take them into the embrace of the Enemy.

I hate to admit it, but pleasure was his invention, not ours. This is one of his most unexpected, inexplicable and despicable tricks. At the beginning we were disgusted enough that he saw fit to create a physical world. When he created two spiritual beings to inhabit it, complete with animal-like "bodies," Our Father Below was suitably scandalized. Then, to top it all, he not only creates this physical world, and populates it with the hairless soul-apes, but he creates them in such a way that they actually take pleasure in being physical.

As hard as it is for you to understand, I must explain that the humans enjoy everything about the physical realm. They like getting wet. They swim and take baths and even enjoy standing in the rain. They smile and take pleasure at sunsets and stars and the moon. They like listening to birds sing and children's laughter. They love the smell of fresh baked bread and flowers and will even inhale the smell of animal manure and call it "good country air."

There's no way around it. The revolting hairless chimps take pleasure in just about every physical aspect of their lives. Furthermore, the Enemy is cheap enough to use their desire to draw them to himself. Do they see a beautiful sunset? He's given them this tacky instinct to thank him for it. The religious ones even thank him for their food—is it a greasy cheeseburger? They eye it with hungry happiness and thank him for it. Horrible.

Here is the most revolting part: the Enemy has given them the most intense pleasure in the most disgusting action of all—breeding. He's even made it into this exalted thing he calls "marriage" so that they really think that through this revolting physical action they are participating in divine love. They even call it "making love."

The thought of this is so utterly repulsive that I can hardly bring myself to mention it. We must admit that all we can really do about it is to limit the pleasure, twist and distort it as much as possible, and use it as a kind of false god which drives their attention away from the Enemy.

It's best to keep them mildly sedated with pleasure. Too much candy makes them sick. As a rule, keep them from any pleasure which requires them to be disciplined or make a sacrifice. Keep their pleasures cheap and cheerful. Junk food rather than fine dining. Trashy TV instead of

Shakespeare or opera. Watching sports rather than playing sports....you know the sort of thing. Their pleasures should become a dull sedative rather than an exhilarating enjoyment of life.

Another tactic is to make them feel guilty and so deny them pleasure altogether. We've been rather successful in using religion itself to accomplish this. Getting religious people to lead pinched, sour, hypocritical and self-righteous lives devoid of any pleasure at all is one of the few consolations we have in the face of the Enemy's inexplicable creation of physical pleasure. Getting them to condemn others for the pleasures they enjoy is even better.

There is more on this topic tomorrow. Get busy and read the chapter "Eat Drink and Be Merry, for Tomorrow You Die" for your homework.

Grimwort, straighten up the furniture and turn out the lights, and when you're done report to my lair, I've got some errands for you. Hurry up, look sharp, toad.

There's the bell. Be gone.

DAY SIXTEEN ~ *Friday*, Second Week of Lent

Day Sixteen - Wednesday, Second Week of Lent

Chamber 101

Slubgrip's voice is heard, barely above a whisper. Background noise of door opening and crowds of students barking, squealing and squeaking.

Thank you, Snort. That's very good news that your student paper has sold out again! Remember, we want a good-sized student revolt. The larger, the better. Then when Professor Knobswart and I suppress it, we'll certainly earn points with Crasston and Snozzle. With any luck a few of the deputies will be sent below, and Knobswart and I will be promoted. I'll make sure I ask for a personal assistant and I can promise you the job, my boy.

He raises his voice:

Worms! Be seated. Did you read "Eat, Drink and Be Merry, for Tomorrow You Die"? Excellent. Hedonism is the love of pleasure, and it is this week's version of relativism. Do you see how they are all connected? First, there is no such thing as truth. Consequently, the only certainty for the miserable bipeds is death. Thirdly: they conclude that since they will soon die they might as well grab as much pleasure as possible.

The problem is, they soon get bored with it. They want something more. This is why philosophy and psychology are so important, dear slugs. When the little brutes get bored with mere pleasure, they start looking for something else. Should they begin to search for some deeper meaning to life or, Gehenna forbid, some kind of religious truth, you must remind them that religion is bunk and there is nothing worth living for but pleasure.

In their more reflective moments this realization will cause them some sadness. They really want something bigger and better to live for, and when they realize there is nothing more than pleasure, they will cling to that pleasure as the only good thing in their life and seek an increasing amount of it. Because it does not ultimately satisfy—convinced that it is the answer—they will seek even more pleasure. You now have the perfect dynamic for a very nice addiction to develop.

You will naturally want to get your patient addicted to something which will destroy his life. Alcohol or drugs are the easy options, but the problem is, this sort of addiction will make your patient miserable and he will always be looking for a way out. Before you know it he will have signed up for a rehab center or joined some horrible self-help group, and the very addiction you lured him into will be the thing which prompts his reversal.

Much better to get your patient addicted to something which is legal, cheap and respectable. Why get him addicted to drugs when you can ruin his life just as effectively with a sex addiction? Why get him addicted to gambling when an addiction to power and prestige can destroy him with the added benefit that he is proud of his accomplishments? Why get your female addicted to alcohol when you might just as well get her addicted to attention, status and the admiration of men? It is far more effective to get your patient addicted to something legal and respectable because they are then unlikely to realize they are addicted.

These are the basics of hedonism, slugs. You see that it's more complicated than merely getting your patient to pig out, get drunk and fornicate. Tomorrow we'll show how science can help keep them distracted before moving on to materialism.

There's the bell. Clear off now and leave me in peace. Grimwort, gather those papers up and have them graded by tomorrow...and clean up those slime trails on the floor, will you? They're disgusting.

DAY SEVENTEEN ~ *Thursday*, Second Week of Lent

Chamber 101

The voice of Slubgrip:

Shanklin, I see that you've got a little gang of so-called friends surrounding you. There's no need to look so sour. If you don't like your situation, change it. When I was in tempter's college we all had a bit of backbone.

Yes, Grimwort, I realize they're slugs and that slugs and worms don't have backbones. Very droll. Isn't he an amusing toad? We really must get you on to the stage, Grimwort. Who knows, you might have a hidden talent for stand-up comedy.

I must address you students for a moment about all the rumbling and grumbling I am hearing. What's wrong with you? When I was your age, I was doing something about the injustice in the world. We had student protests. We brought down the administration with a few well-planned sit-ins. If you got together and did something about your complaints, you might find a few faculty and staff would join you. There now, enough rabble-rousing.

This week I have been trying to explain why the humans enjoy the disgusting physical realm they live in and what you can do about it. The pleasure they enjoy is our worst nightmare, but it is also our greatest tool. If the Enemy made them to live in the physical realm, one of the best things we can do is keep them there.

If we can keep them convinced that there is nothing beyond what they can see, touch, taste, smell and hear, then we'll have them just where we want them. Do you see, slugs? This is always what we do best. Take what the Enemy has given, then cut it and twist it. He wants them to be physical and enjoy the physical world? Very well, we must make sure that they have nothing *but* the physical world.

One of the tasks of popular culture is to get them so involved in the physical things of this world that they lose all perception of the spiritual realm. One of the ways to do this is to help them see that the only thing they can believe in is what can be scientifically tested. This assumption that the only valid knowledge is scientific knowledge is called scientism.

The way to promote this within popular culture is to set up the Enemy's viewpoint as hopelessly unscientific. An excellent way to do this is to take the first chapters of the Book of Genesis, which is a sad little Hebrew story about the Enemy supposedly creating the world in six days. Never let the cretins learn that the story was always just that—a story— and it was never meant to be a scientific account. Instead, show them how ridiculous it is. Get them to focus on whether it really is sinful to eat an apple and point out that it is all a silly fairy tale about naked ladies and talking snakes.

Fuel the fire with some literature from Christian fundamentalists who insist that the Genesis story *is* a scientific account, and promote the theory of evolution to show how the religious account is foolishness. By the way, don't allow them to see that the theory of evolution is just another kind of story about the creation of the world. Because it's a scientific story, they should assume that the theory has been tested and verified.

You need to make science the new religion. Its truths become the new dogma. This is done most effectively within popular culture—not in the science lab. We don't want them to become truly questioning, objective scientific researchers. That would be a disaster.

Instead you must get your patient to simply assume that science has disproved religion. Suddenly they will see all the miracle stories they learned in Sunday School as fairy tales. Once they come to believe that these stories are make-believe, it's only a short hop before the "truths" they learned in religion class can also be written off as well-meaning fairy tales devised by spinster Sunday School teachers.

Every form of the media and education should be used to reinforce the conviction in their minds that science has disproved religion. Every article, news report and television documentary should be written according to this underlying assumption. If it is buried deep enough, it will be considered an unshakeable and universal truth.

This is the way with popular culture. Keep our message below the surface. Keep them distracted with the flickering images so they don't have the time or inclination to think about what we are really saying.

You need to read the next chapter, worms. It's called "Philosophy and Fakery." It will back up my lecture today, and give us something to work on for the rest of the week.

A bells clangs.

DAY EIGHTEEN ~ *Friday,* Second Week of Lent

Chamber 101

Moans, groans and complaining are heard. Mock snoring and whistling. A high voice calls out, "Boooring!!"

Slubgrip's voice:

Grimwort, give me my tablets and that glass of fumes, will you? And get them to come to order. Their constant bickering doesn't help my migraine.

Be quiet, will you! Come to attention or you will pay for it later. Fail this course and you will be rewarded with a dinner invitation to the Master's banqueting rooms. I've been there, and I can assure you there is always room for escargots on the menu.

We are talking about keeping the humans' attention on the physical realm. Scientism—the idea that scientifically verified knowledge is the only knowledge—helps, but the problem is that, if they think it through for even a moment, they will realize that even science reveals that there are more things than can be explained with the scientific method. Whether it's a book on psychology or quantum physics, their minds start opening up to all sorts of dangerous non-physical aspects of reality.

Should your patient start exploring the non-physical realm and start imagining that there is "more in heaven and earth than his philosophy has dreamt of," who knows where it will end up? He's in dangerous territory. The best way to bring him back very quickly to the physical realm is to remind him that he doesn't have enough money. That's right. Money. It's amazing how quickly money worries bring them right back to earth.

Turning their thoughts to money is an excellent way to keep their minds on the material realm, and worries about money can quickly be turned to greed.

An addiction to money is very much to be desired, but they mustn't see themselves as greedy. It is more satisfying to get them to see their obsession with material goods as simply being "prudent" or "cautious." When they see poor people, plant in their minds the idea that "those people" haven't taken responsibility for themselves and that they deserve to be poor.

Fight hard against the idea in your patient's mind that he might give some of his money to the poor. This is one of the Enemy's most wearisome projects. He wants his half-breeds to give their money away. For some time we thought it was because he wanted a nauseating new temple built for "his glory" or he wanted the poor humans to have better housing or food.

We were wrong. As usual he had an ulterior motive. He commanded his half-breeds to give their money away not because the poor needed food or the church needed a new roof. He told them to give their money so they wouldn't be addicted to their wealth. It was a dirty trick, and at first we didn't understand it.

Make them hold on to their cash. The more they cling to it, the more they will be bound to the material realm. The more they trust in the security of their riches, the more they will belong to us. The more they hold on to their money, the more their money will hold on to them, and the more their money holds on to them, the more we hold on to them. Be lampreys and leeches, my dear fellows. Be lampreys and leeches.

Once they start giving, watch out. You will have your patient firmly in your grasp, busily counting his investments, cash and holding, then before you know it he's learned to be generous. As he starts giving away his loot you will gaze in horror to discover that he has been liberated from your grasp. He's become aware of a new dimension to life; he's woken up to the reality of the spiritual realm, and has turned from being a sour old miser to a joyful and free spirit.

Believe me, such transformations are truly horrible to behold. Be warned. You can lose your patient in a flash, and when that happens, the consequences will be swift and your invitation to dinner will be delivered in person by the Flancks.

Gecko will be here as guest speaker tomorrow. He'll tell you all about finance, and on Sunday my dear friend Snoot will discuss shopping. I think you will find both of them entertaining and informative. For Monday's lesson, read the chapter "Love and Death."

Class dismissed.

DAY NINETEEN ~ *Saturday,* Second Week of Lent

Chamber 101

A boisterous and bellowing voice is heard. It is the tempter Gecko.

Okay, guys. Sit down and shut up. Slubgrip probably told you, I'm Gecko. Maybe you've heard of me.

Straight to the point. Bottom line: greed is good. Greed motivates people. It makes them get things done. The hungry animal fights best. Know what I mean?

Look, I didn't get where I am by sitting around contemplating my navel. I see the world the way it is and I accept it. I'm not going around whining and crying like a big baby. You tell your patient to be realistic. The pie is only so big, and the question is, "How big a piece of that pie is he going to get?"

It's not rocket science, fellas. The way you get ahead is by rolling a few heads. You can't make an omelet without breaking a few eggs, and you can't make a million without breaking a few banks. Listen. Only dummies break a bank with a gun. The way to really rob a bank is to be a banker. Do it legal. How do you make it legal? It's easy. By changing the law. How do you change the law? Change the politician. How do you change the politician? Buy him. Everybody has his price. Believe me.

Once your patient realizes this, the rest is cake. You got a problem with somebody? Find out his price. This is the way the world turns: it turns on a dime. You get it?

Let me tell you the four basics: prosperity, power, prestige and pleasure. That's all that matters. They're the four "P" words. Memorize them, slugs: prosperity, power, prestige and pleasure. Get your little monkey men to plug into the four "P's"—then you'll come out on top.

Number one? Prosperity. It's about money, boys. Loads of money. If your patient gets squeamish, let him think that it's not about money, it's about freedom. Yeah, sure.

Number two. Power. This means coming out on top. Not just winning, but beating the other guy. Tell your hairless chimp that he needs to win. No place for losers. He needs to beat the other guy so that guy will show him some respect. Show him how to cheat and undercut the other guy. If he starts being a crybaby and whining "cheaters never win," tell him he's wrong. Cheaters *do* win. Just look around. Cheaters win all the time.

Numero tres. Prestige. What's the point of the prosperity and power if nobody appreciates it? Teach your boys how to strut their stuff a little. Hey, nothing vulgar, right? Teach them to be classy about it. Tell him to get a good tailor and join the right country club. Get him to belong to the high-class businessmen's group like the masons. Send his kids to the good schools and make him respectable. Nothing better than to see some of our high-class broads and their menfolk swanning about thinking they're the cat's meow when you and I know they're a bunch of crooks. Even better—get them to join some high-class church like the Episcopalians.

Last one—pleasure. I'm talking about the good life. Get him to go for it and don't hold back.

If he gets a little bit snooty about this, tell him he's being a sissy. Don't let him wimp out on you. Kick his butt if you need to. If he gets squeamish about cutting a dirty deal or jumping in front of the other guy or cheating on his wife, remind him that if he doesn't get his loot first, somebody else will get his grubby mitts in there ahead of him.

There's no sugar daddy in the sky who's going to make it right for them. There's nobody else who's going to look out for number one so they'd better get used to it.

Listen, fellas, the last thing you want to tell the little brute is this— that you're doing it for his own good. If he's a follower of that lily-livered hippie from Galilee he'll try to wimp out on you. If he gets all worried, tell him he can use the money to do some good one day.

Hell, tell him he can leave it all to Mother Teresa when he dies. Tell him he's going to do a lot of good with all that money. Flash the loot in front of their eyes, boys, and remember everybody has their price.

Everybody.

DAY TWENTY ~ *Sunday*, Second Week of Lent

Chamber 101

A cultured, feminine voice with a sweet Southern accent is heard. It is the tempter Snoot:

Good morning, boys! Good morning, Grimwort!

I'm so delighted that my dear friend Slubgrip has invited me to say a few words about materialism and its wonderful effects in those dear, sad, little creatures called humans.

I just think they're so adorable sometimes! Dear little monkey faces they have, and to think the Enemy has given them eternal souls! What a sad, funny little experiment of his!

May I sit down? I always get rather weary around this time of the week, don't you? It's that awful smell that seeps down from above.

Let's get down to business, shall we? Slubgrip has asked me to give you a few pointers about the practicalities of materialism. What we're talking about here is shopping. Oh, it's easy enough in the early days to get your patients all a-goggle over the pretty things they can buy, but the real delight in this area of temptation is not simply to get them to buy everything in sight, but to understand *why* the poor imbeciles buy things.

You see, my dear slugs, the Enemy doesn't really mind if the little monkey children have nice things. That's why it's your job to understand *why* they want things, and to encourage their materialism in the right way.

Let me give you an example. Let's say my patient, Dolly Bird, wants a new hat. I don't mind if she gets a new hat, and the Enemy doesn't mind if she gets a new hat. What I want, however, is for her to make sure that her new hat is nicer and more expensive than her neighbor's new hat. Consequently it is not about a new hat at all, but about her getting one up on her neighbor.

Furthermore, by whispering some sweet nothings in her ear, I can get her not only to buy the most expensive hat, but get her to feel that she is a unique and wonderful person for being able not only to afford such a hat, but to have such fine taste. It the hat is actually hideous, the little game is even more delightful.

Let's say one of the young humans wants a new car. There is nothing at all wrong with his having a new car. Your job is to make sure the poor meathead buys a car he can't afford in order to make himself think he is attractive to women, or in order to show off. The acquisition of a car or a hat—or virtually anything—becomes a source for vanity, snobbery, greed, envy and pride. You see? We use the material possessions (which are quite harmless in themselves) to accomplish a greater goal.

The most delightful use of material possessions is to make your patient think that he or she is being admired because of their belongings. Of course this is a total illusion, Very few of the monkey men respect another one because of what they have. In fact, it is far more likely that they will despise the other one for having more than they do.

Nevertheless, the poor sweet fools think other people admire them for their big house, flashy car or fancy wardrobe. Once you get your patient to start buying things because they are convinced that others admire them because of their fine things, you are well on the way to a nice pattern of addictive behavior.

Now this is *real* materialism: when a patient starts to use their material possessions as an artificial means of buying respect and admiration, and what is respect and admiration except another form of love? Do you see how sad and pitiful the poor little monkey men are? They always need reassurance, bless their hearts. Always desperate for affection like pathetic puppies.

My dear worms, it is most gratifying to see them behave in such an infantile manner. It is a mystery we cannot understand, but it seems the Enemy has made them to love and be loved—but they are willing to settle for a new dress, a fancier car, a trophy kitchen or a beach house.

When you get your patient to that state, keep them there. Keep them sedated by their possessions while, at the same time you keep them in a quiet state of desperation, constantly buying more and more things that are increasingly expensive so they can get that little kick of self-approval.

Why you wouldn't believe how many of the poor cretins we've ensnared in this way. "Shop until you drop?" I should say so! Drop right into our Father's house.

Thank you so much for your attention and insights! How nice to have been with you today! Remember all that you've learned from me…and remember…

Our Father is watching, and I don't want to be downstairs asking, "Guess who's coming to dinner?" now do I?

DAY TWENTY-ONE ~ *Monday,* Third Week of Lent

Chamber 101

The voice of Slubgrip in a hoarse whisper:

Snort, my boy, you're doing a pretty fine job so far. Our little protest is moving along nicely, and Knobswart has got his classes to a fever pitch. How is Shanklin doing with that petition? He'll probably need some help. Once we get things simmering along, it will only take a crisis to set off the wildfire. Then I call in the Flancks and suppress the riot and Knobby and I—and of course you, my dear fellow—will come out on top. And there's another thing…Ah, best be quiet now. I'll tell you later. Take your seat—here they come.

In a louder voice:

Come in, worms. Come in. I'm afraid our class today couldn't be on a more boring and revolting topic. Sex and the human beings. I know it is a subject you find both extremely dull and repugnant, but the hairless apes get all excited by it—like dogs drooling for their supper.

We have been explaining how important it is to keep your patient wrapped up only in the physical world. Keeping your patient obsessed with sexual pleasure is one of the ways you will be most successful in this matter. I know how disgusting it is to be discussing their reproductive functions, but we must brace ourselves and get to work. No sense being squeamish.

First of all, realize that this is where the Enemy made his big—and I mean *really big*—mistake. He created them to have pleasure in reproducing.

They obviously enjoy rutting like pigs, but let me put it straight to you. There is one simple, nauseating reason for their sexual behavior: it is for them to produce children. His servants load it all up with talk of "love" and "mutual self-giving," but that's all window dressing. When it comes to human sexuality, it is all quite simple. The Enemy wants the world to be overrun by the vermin. Therefore he made it pleasurable for them to mate. Furthermore, he wants their mating to be done within marriage so the little brats they produce will have a secure and "happy" home.

Here is his weak point: the miserable mongrels find his restrictions unbearable. Being married to one person for life and never mating with anyone else is unthinkable for them. Nowadays they're not too happy with the production of children, either.

This is where popular culture has such an important part to play. In all that we do, we have the simple task of reinforcing the idea that sex is no more than a party game. In television shows, movies and music, keep pounding home the idea that sex has no connection with pregnancy. You don't need to make it all pornographic (we'll have a session on that later). Instead show attractive, intelligent and funny young people getting together. After the first meeting all you need to do is show them going through the same front door, sipping coffee and then cut to the next scene with them having breakfast together. Do you see how easy a bit of subtlety is, my dear fellows?

The idea is to make fornication, adultery and free for all sexual activity seem like the normal, clean-cut, all-American way of living. Never let them see that they are behaving like brute beasts in heat. Never let them see the treachery, betrayal, selfishness and crudity of their behavior. You want them to equate their own sexual adventures with the glamor, beauty and wealth of the media stars we put in front of them.

Never let them see the reality of their own sexual experience. They mustn't see that the real girl they're with is overweight, insecure and has acne. Never let them see that the boy they've gone with is a weedy dysfunctional drunk with no prospects. Most of all, never let them see that their unwholesome sexual act is fleeting and unsatisfying.

If their unhappiness leads them to question their behavior, you may lose them very quickly. Instead you want to whisper in their ear that their sexual encounter was unsatisfactory because they lack physical prowess or "technique." The other ploy when they become dissatisfied with their sexual party games is to tell them that they simply haven't found the ideal partner. You want them to consider sex to be like a game of tennis. It's a fun as long as you have an good partner. This is where the media becomes useful again. Once the brute is unhappy with his or her "sex life," set him or her out on a quest to find the "right partner."

Before long you'll have them out every night like a tomcat—always on the move, and never in love. With a little bit of luck and skill, your patient will approach middle age alone and lonely with a beer belly and a little black book full of crossed-out names. Once his tomcat behavior has led him to total loneliness, with a bottle of pills or a pistol you might just push him over the brink into the sudden plunge into Our Father's house.

You can work the same trick with the females, and with them the result is even more delightful. They spend their twenties "sleeping around." Then when they hit their thirties, they'll continue the behavior because now it has become a habit. They still think they'll get married and have a nice house in the suburbs and have three children and a dog, and bake cookies for after school. The delight when they wake up one morning in their late thirties and realize that they've lost any chance at their dream is simply too delicious for words.

If your patient becomes disenchanted and disappointed with sex, make them believe that the reason is not because they have had too much "free sex" but because they have not had enough.

You simply must not allow this basic, underlying assumption to be challenged. You must work on it ceaselessly. Through pop music, magazines, websites, advertising, television shows, movies, games, books, novels—every outlet in popular culture must give the same message: that it's sexual party time and everything is fun and anything goes.

Class dismissed. For tomorrow, read the next chapter in the text: "Porn and Pawns."

Grimwort, hop down to the Lavatory and get me cup of lava and one of those harlot honeybuns.

Snort? Hang on a minute there. What I didn't get to tell you at the beginning of class is that I have been working on an idea that I think will please you. President Thornblade is looking for a part-time administrative assistant, and I think I can get you the job. Are you interested? Good. Good. I'll keep you posted.

DAY TWENTY-TWO ~ *Tuesday,* Third Week of Lent

Chamber 101

Voice of Slubgrip:

Worms, slugs, flukes—all of you, come to order. I see from the attendance record that Shanklin has transferred over to Advanced Finance and Fraud with Professor Grubb. I wish him success, but I doubt if the cowardly worm is good for anything more than tempting teens to waste time playing video games.

I understand he has complained to the administration of being bullied in this class. The crybaby should know that Commissioner Crasston considers hazing to be all part of the training here at Bowelbages. It builds character. It's easy. If you are being bullied, you deserve it. Get over it.

In the last session I tried to impress upon you the need to keep hammering home to the hairless bipeds the truth that sex is simply a party game. Today the topic is pornography.

The danger with your patient playing around with sex as a party game is that he might actually fall in love. The Enemy is always at work. Even when we think a patient is going down the right track and living a life of continual one-night stands, you find that suddenly he actually falls for the girl or she for him, and before you know it they're talking about marriage and cute little babies.

This is why pornography can be much more successful. You may be somewhat disappointed that you can't get him out clubbing and sleeping around every weekend. But a pornography addiction will be far more long-lasting, and its results far more dependable and satisfactory. You will have your man's mind and imagination.

Having control of his lower regions may be more exciting, but the results are unpredictable and often very displeasing. On the other hand, getting him addicted to pornography and therefore never letting him come close to a real relationship, love and marriage, will lead to some very satisfying results.

I don't have much more to say about pornography, except to point out with some pleasure that we have most assuredly won this battle. The pornography industry in the United States, for example, has a higher gross income than many developing countries. It's simply huge, dear slugs. It's everywhere. Pornography is no longer associated with the furtive visit to the magazine store, the hasty grab from the top shelf, the discreet brown paper bag and the hurry home to enjoy the illicit lust. Instead the average man can watch sexual activities which his grandfather could scarcely even imagine in the privacy of his study or workshop at the flick of a switch.

You may be thinking that pornography is for men only. It is and it isn't. It is true that the females of the species are usually not drawn to pornography. If they look at it, they're more likely to be repulsed—"Yucch! That's sick!" or just curious—"Goodness, how did she get into that position without hurting her back?!" This is because the male of the species likes to look. The female likes to be looked at. She wants to be admired and loved. Once you understand this, flukes, you've got the key. Just as the man fantasizes about his sexual exploits, the woman fantasizes about being loved, needed and admired.

Pornography for females therefore takes its appropriate form. They don't look at pictures about sex, they read stories about love. I'm talking about "romance novels," squirm worms. You might think them anodyne and dull—harmless, even—but some of our best authors are making the heroines increasingly unchaste.

The women in these books "make their own sexual choices." In addition, our agents are making the love scenes more and more sexually explicit. Here's the delightful detail: the female of the species may well consume three or four "romance novels" in a month. The simpering little lipstick feeds her imagination and fantasizes about being a "sexually liberated woman." She's locked into a fantasy world of sex just as much as the man looking at pornography, but because she doesn't look at dirty pictures she thinks nothing of it.

This is the crunch—to get both the males and females locked into a fantasy world of sex. We want them to live in an unreal world where all the women are overblown and oversexed and all the men are unbelievably handsome. When they go looking for a spouse, they'll be frustrated. Because such people never existed in the first place, your stupid little biped will go on an endless quest looking for an ideal (but nonexistent) partner they think will make them happy. Whenever they meet a real man or woman they will reject them as "not good enough," never for one moment imagining that they themselves are "not good enough".

This is your aim. Use pornography in all its forms to draw your patient into a fantasy world. Cut him off from reality, slugs. Overload his imagination with lies and you will incapacitate his will.

A bell clangs.

Class dismissed.

DAY TWENTY-THREE ~ *Wednesday,* Third Week of Lent

Knobswart's Office

Slubgrip's voice is heard.

Knobby, may I come in? Thank you. Thank you.

I must say your speech to the faculty members was just perfect. You were able to express total loyalty to Crasston and Snozzle while undermining everyone's confidence in their leadership. I especially loved your line, "We are all called to be loyal foot soldiers and not to question their decisions—even when we can see that they are self-serving and incompetent."

May I make a suggestion? I told my boy Snort that the rebellion was only a mock rebellion so that you and I would step in and work with the Flancks to suppress it and thereby gain the approval of Thornblade, Crasston and Snozzle. Snort is under the impression that you and I, Knobby, will be promoted and then give him a leg up. He doesn't realize that the rebellion is for real. To make sure he doesn't get any further information from us I've finagled a spot for him in the President's office. It gets him out of the way while at the same time it gives us an ear and an eye in Thornblade's office.

Let's check how we're doing. You've got Brine from Propaganda and Froth and Shrank from Psychology organized, and they've each got three classes behind them. I've managed to persuade Strump to come on board.

She says the Flancks hate Crasston, and we could have nearly half of them on our side... *and* they've got keys to the arsenal. I've got Grime, Zelnick, Sturbage and Thrallspot to bring their classes, so between us we've got enough to launch the takeover.

We need to look for an appropriate flashpoint to set things off. Then you and I can call in the Flancks under the pretense of quashing the rebellion, and if the wind is blowing in our direction we can turn the whole thing. You and your four classes can march on Crasston's office. Sturbage, Thrallspot and Zelnick can take Snozzle, and I'll go with Grime and his class and head for Thornblade's office. In the meantime Strump will bring around the Flancks who are loyal. They'll disarm Thornblade's Flancks, help neutralize Crasston and Snozzle, and the coup should be over in a matter of minutes.

What's that, Knobby? You want to march on Thornblade's office? My dear Knobswart, you don't trust me? After all we've been through together? Yes, of course I remember saying that you would be president in place of Thornblade, and that's precisely what will happen, but surely you must see that if you march on Thornblade's office and then take his position it will look simply too grandiose and ambitious.

Believe me, Knobby, it will be far better for *me* to take Thornblade. Then once the coup is completed, I will come out on the balcony and give a speech along the lines of "We have all rallied in the cause of freedom to overthrow the tyrants, and lest you think I wish to be president...I am now stepping down." We'll make sure the crowds call for you, and I will welcome you to take office.

It is really rather hurtful that you don't trust me, Knobby. You needn't bring up that old rumor about me trying to take you down when we were working together in the prison sector. I never plotted against you. It was a vicious lie. The others lied about me to you in order to destroy our friendship.

Of course I'll propose you for President at that point, my dear fellow! You can be President and I'll take over Crasston and Snozzle's posts in Security and Detention. We'll make a splendid team, Knobby. Just like old times!

So we're agreed? Good! Good. Why not come around this evening to drink on it? I've got some snacks—crunchy deep fried traitor's skin. Just the thing with a bottle of delicious bubbly blonde I've been saving for a special occasion. Three o'clock sharp? See you then!

DAY TWENTY-FOUR ~ *Thursday,* Third Week of Lent

Chamber 101

The voice of Slubgrip:

Slimetoads, you may not understand why we spend a whole week on the disgusting subject of sex, but it's not really about what they do with the middle part of their bodies—we couldn't care less about that.

The reason we tempt them to sexual misbehavior is not that we take any particular pleasure in their bodily functions—although I realize some of you think it's all very smutty and funny…Do try to be serious for once—try to respect Grimwort's values. He's such a very prim and pious tempter, aren't you, Grimwort? So very prissy and strict. Turns up his nose at the mere mention of sexuality, don't you, old toad?

Guffaws, howls, laughter and hoots.

No, we tempt them to indulge their sexual desires because their sexuality is linked to something which is far more dangerous to us than the mere fact of them enjoying themselves for a few squalid moments.

The sexual urge is linked to something the Enemy calls "marriage." This odious invention of his seems to be part of his plan from the very beginning when he first established those two bone-headed Neanderthals in that jungle they call "the Garden of Eden." He created the man and woman to be in a sick, symbiotic relationship in which they depend on one another. It's quite creepy—all rather parasitical—which at least you tapeworms will understand…

The Enemy has invested a huge amount in this unhealthy relationship. Through this he wants the miserable half-breeds to learn how to "love" one another—although what that's supposed to mean we have yet to figure out. For all I can make out he intends them to feed on one another and become even more dependent on the other person until they can't live without one another. Then, even worse, through their interdependence he wants them to learn how to "love" him. This is what I find so degrading and disgusting about the Enemy—he's always fawning all over everybody like a puppy—desperate, just desperate for attention and this thing he calls "love."

Well, my dear slugs, believe it or not, he has designed it all in such a way that what they do with their genitals is all tied in with this master plan he has for them. It's inextricably linked with this sentimental nonsense called "love and marriage." I wish it were not so, but it is.

Imagine the low-down, dirty, conniving tricksy nature of it all! The Enemy has no pride. He'll stoop down to the lowest of the low—using even their organs of waste and breeding to attempt to weave in his horrible make-believe of "love, light and life."

That's why we distort the sexual act whenever possible. It's really an attack on this horrible invention of his called marriage. If we can get a young man addicted to pornography, masturbation and serial fornication, he'll find it harder to commit to marriage—and that's the real aim.

If we can get a girl to go with every boy who comes along and treat sex like a game, she'll be unable to make a solid marriage. If we get them to treat every relationship as a fleeting pleasure, they will not have the ability, inclination or self-discipline to even attempt marriage.

All of our work in this area is about the destruction of marriage. Take the whole long list of wearisome sins which the poor bipeds find so irresistible: adultery, fornication, rape, homosexuality, self-titillation, sexual fantasies—you name it—they're only good because they help us to undermine and destroy marriage.

Tomorrow we'll discuss how to dissolve that horrible institution of the Enemy's called the family.

Loud groans and moans.

Yes, I know it is dreary, but it must be done. Grimwort, get this paperwork over to Demerits and Discipline. Hop to it, toad.

Shuffling of books and bodies as students leave class.

Snort, my boy, do you have a minute? Come over here....That job I was telling you about? It's a green light. Report to President Thornblade's office on Monday and they'll get you started. May I just say, Snort, that it would be very helpful if you kept your eyes and ears wide open when you're there. I thrive on information and I'll meet with you from time to time to find out what's going on. Nothing sinister, of course, just keeping up to date and watching my back—as you have to do around here.

DAY TWENTY-FIVE ~ *Friday,* Third Week of Lent

Chamber 101

The voice of Slubgrip:

Come to order, you horrible worms. Come to order! My head is splitting! Quiet! Ohh, the headaches! Where are my tablets and my fumes, Grimwort?

Now, listen to me, will you? Yesterday I explained how we use the sexual drive to destroy marriage. Furthermore, marriage with all its squishy and disgusting sexual activity is linked with something even more disgusting: infant human beings.

The Enemy has designed it all in such a way that the hairless bipeds actually *want* more of their own kind. The female goes all starry-eyed and has an instinct to breed. She wants little brats who not only grow inside her body, but then come out like some obscene parasite. Even worse, once they are born they feed on her—sucking milk from her breasts—like piglets grunting and snorting to suckle the sow.

I can see how disgusted you are by the sheer physicality of all this. It's revolting! Horrible! Absolutely vile! And to think that the Enemy sent his own heir to become one of the mewling, puking, sucking, toothless little squids is totally and utterly beyond me.

His plan is for each one of these revolting miniature beasts to grow up into a new inhabitant of heaven. That's right, Incredible as it may seem, he's populating heaven with the hairless piglets. He's breeding them to take your place and mine! He's breeding them to become his slaves. That's what he's doing! He's always longing for more adoring sycophants and he's always coming up with new ideas to create yet more armies of drooling, idiot children to serve him night and day.

It's sickening. Just sickening. And he says *we're* proud! What could be more proud (and sick I might add) than wanting an endless number of dependent, adoring nasty little children? It's sheer megalomania. That's what it is.

It's all built into his seemingly harmless creation called "the family." The rot starts there, and it continues. Before we knew it at the very beginning he sneaked the idea in with those naive Neanderthals Adam and Eve.

Step on it, slugs. Destroy it. Destroy the children and destroy the family and destroy marriage. All of it stinks. It stinks like the nauseating flowers of heaven. It stinks like the revoltingly rotten and overripe fruit of the orchards above. Trample it. Kill the children. Stop marriage. Obliterate this artificial and sentimental emotion they call "love"!

First of all, you must get rid of the idea that marriage is for life. We've managed to make divorce quick and easy. You make sure your patient sees it that way. He or she doesn't need to stay married to someone who has turned out to be unpleasant. That line about "for better or for worse"? They must forget about that. With divorce we get a triple benefit. A marriage is broken, the spouses usually feel self-righteous about it, and they break a solemn vow they made before the Enemy without giving it much more than a moment's thought.

The next tactic to destroy the family is to separate the sexual act from breeding. Get them to believe that the sexual action is only for their own pleasure. Make contraception universal. Promote it all—rubber gadgets, pills and potions, douches and foams and wires and coils—whatever will stop a brat from being conceived, use it. Use sex education in schools to hammer home the fundamental understanding that sex has nothing to do with babies.

If some of the toothless squids are still conceived, rip them from the womb. We don't want abortion to be safe, legal and rare. We want an abortion clinic on every street corner. We'd have them in every pharmacy if possible. Safe? Who cares if it's safe or not? Poison the brats. Cut them up in pieces and suck them out! This is our triumph!

What a delight, dear slugs! What a delight! There are very few rewards in this work, I can tell you, but a visit to the abortion mill is one of those times when you know the sweet smell of victory. When you see the little horrible human lives squelched out, strangled, poisoned, dismembered and thrown away—oh what a wonderful spectacle it is!

And to think that we have gotten them to do so and believe that what they are doing is civilized because their doctors do this in clean clinics wearing white coats, all under the protection of the law.

Finally, destroy the family by destroying the children. Attack their innocence. Corrupt them early. Teach them to distrust and disobey their parents. Make them long to grow up, but only give them immature adults as role models.

It's the weekend, slugs, and there is no rest for the dreary. At least you have some entertaining guest lecturers. Tomorrow Strump will be here to discuss the predatory female, and on Sunday Flambeaux will lecture you on the subversion of masculinity.

Both of them have their own line of attack, and I think you'll find them amusing.

Grimwort, where have you put my cape and fedora? Hop to it, toad.

DAY TWENTY-SIX ~ *Saturday,* Third Week of Lent

Chamber 101

Door closes. Bell clanging. Grunts, squeaks and growls as the demon students enter.

A brisk and brusque, deep female voice is heard. The crack of a small whip against leather. It is the tempter Strump:

C'mon, chaps. Look lively.

The crack of a whip. A shriek followed by a snarl.

No need to get nasty, my boy. I gave you a crack with the whip because you were slinking along there at a snail's pace. Move it!

Let's get one thing straight right away. The Enemy has constructed a ridiculous myth about the female humans. I'm sure you remember the fairy tale about the naked woman and man in the garden? You know, they're not supposed to eat an apple, but along comes a talking snake. Anything wrong, so far?

That's right, Slurge—Our Father Below doesn't like to be humiliated by being called a lowly snake. A magnificent dragon is one of his preferred manifestations, but why else is the silly myth so insulting? Anyone? Hello? Helloooo! Wakey wakey! Why is the myth insulting?

That's right, Snort, it insults the woman. She's portrayed as a silly bimbo who falls into the temptation trap. From then on it's all her fault. She's got to pay the price, first by having pain in childbirth, then by being the submissive wifey-doormat, barefoot and pregnant in the kitchen for ever and ever world without end!

Grubs. Worms. Are you there? Do you see how the so-called "Father in heaven" has slanted the whole thing in his favor? It's not only him who pretends to be the big guy, but all the human males get to be the big guy, too, and who's supposed to be there to have their supper on the table and be their submissive little mates?

That's right, Snort—the poor females. The whole thing is a set-up by "Our Father Who Art in Heaven." That fake Father in heaven who says he's loving, but spends all his time oppressing women is very different from Our Father Below who wants nothing more than to liberate women from the chains clapped on them by all the Jewish guys with long beards.

Your job is to help the female humans reclaim their rightful place. This is where popular culture helps. Through newspapers, websites, magazines, books, and most importantly in the universities and colleges, we've been able to put the female human on the right track.

Their grandmothers were trained to wait at home demurely for "the gentleman caller." No more of that stuff, boys. Now the girls are in charge. We get them started in middle school. As soon as the hormones hit, they start hitting on the boys. It's pretty smart to see a seventh-grade girl stalk a boy. We get her to text him, write notes, pester him on Facebook and send him emails. She gangs up on the boy with her friends, putting notes in his locker, hanging around at his sports activities and using emotional blackmail and sexual pressure to get him to "go out with her" or "be her boyfriend" when the dumb kid wants no more than to have some free time to play football or frisbee with his pals.

As the girl gets older she may start to think that being predatory isn't getting her the right kind of boyfriend. Only the boys who don't mind being dominated or the boys who see her as a quick lay hang around. So what do you do when she starts doubting?

Tell her that she wasn't successful because she wasn't being predatory enough. She needs to be even more aggressive. What's that, Snort? Yes, not only more aggressive, but more sexually permissive. Whisper in her ear that she is not succeeding because she's not giving him enough sex. With a bit of finesse you'll have the girl behaving like a prostitute and she'll be proud of it—thinking that she's "in charge of her own sexual choices."

This is where it gets interesting, boys. We use popular culture to get the female to copulate with as many men as possible without having a child. What we want is a woman who is on the prowl—looking for the best man, but never realizing that the best men think she's nothing more than a trollop.

The little cow will end up hurt and rejected by most men, and then it's only a short push to get her to be permanently angry at all men and thus lose the chance of what the Enemy calls "love" forever.

That's the game plan, slugs. Make it work.

A bell clangs. Doors opening and closing. Crack of whip. The sound of a yelp. Strump's voice:

Move along, you pitiful excuse for a tempter, or you'll feel more than the bite of the whip.

DAY TWENTY-SEVEN ~ *Sunday,* Fourth Week of Lent

Chamber 101

A soft, gentle voice is heard. It is the demon Flambeaux. He speaks smoothly and affects a stammer.

Gentleworms! Gentleworms! P..p...puleeze!

What must I do to g.g.get your attention? Oh, my...*Giggles*... you are a tease, aren't you!

That's better. Now let me see. What do you think of old Slubgrip? Isn't he just the w.w.wiliest old fox? I think the world of him. So charming. So debonair in his silk waistcoat, don't you think? So polished and urbane. Such finely buffed horns, such soft hands and polished nails! But you must watch him, my dears. His ch.ch.charm conceals his fangs. He's very experienced, and I must warn you—always think twice before you accept his invitation to d.d.dinner. When he says he has a place for you it may be between the first and second course.

Anyway, my dears, Slubgrip has asked me to come along and give you a little conference about the menfolk. I know there is a lot of talk here below about how disgusting the human beings are, but you know I rather like them. When prepared properly they're really rather scrumptious.

Let's get down to business. When we're talking about popular culture, one of our great successes has been the erosion of m.m.masculinity. What I mean by "masculinity" are all those beefy, athletic, soldier types. So f.f.full of testosterone, my dears, so brimming with a sort of gorilla-like brutishness. All b.b.beards, bristles and bruises. Uggh! Always so ready to hit someone or shoot a gun. So ready to kill an animal and cook outside. It's not n.n.nice my dears, it's positively N.N.Neanderthal.

What we've been able to do in recent years is domesticate the b.b.barbarians. You see, all this is linked with that unspeakable concept of the Enemy's called "patriarchy." Because they can father children, the thick-headed baboons think themselves quite special.

They march about giving orders and expecting everyone to jump just because they're the so-called head of the family. We must stop it. No more of this "Father knows best" m.m.military nonsense.

If you have a male patient, you've got your work cut out for you. First of all, make him feel guilty for being masculine. Make him feel bad if he comes home from work and doesn't immediately put on an apron, clean the house, change diapers and make supper. Make him feel guilty for smoking a pipe, spending too much time in the workshop or study or enjoying a football game in the "rec room" with a few beers and a few b.b.buddies.

Work with their women's tempters to nag them into being milquetoast mama's boys. The aim is to undermine their caveman concepts of masculinity. The women need to get the men to be "more sympathetic." They haven't a clue, poor m.m.meatheads, what their emotions are about; so make them feel guilty for that, too. Convince them that they ought to be more "in touch with their feelings."

Feminism has helped us enormously in this way. It's one of Our Father Below's b.b.better jokes. He calls it "feminism" while getting the women to be masculine and the men feminine. It is no mistake that this pleasing ideology has been developed hand-in-hand with the promotion of homosexualism. This has b.b.been another one of our great successes.

I am not dealing with the question of whether or not your patient is attracted to people of the same sex. That is a complex area of temptation which is covered by Dr. Thrallspot's Sexuality and Socialization course. What I am referring to is homosexuality's influence on the culture. The idea my dears, is to use every aspect of p.p.popular culture to convince the humans that homosexuality is p.p.perfectly natural.

Homosexuals must be portrayed as charming, intelligent, good-looking and witty. Even though they are a very small minority, you must load popular culture outlets with them. While you are portraying them as mainstream, you mustn't forget to play exactly the opposite note and also portray them as a wounded and persecuted minority. Use both tactics. No one will notice.

The b.b.bottom line is this, my dears: Destroy marriage by destroying m.m.masculinity. Do it however you can. What we don't want your human to do is to become a fully functional, active, red-b.b.blooded, married, b.b.breeding human male. Yucch! Is there anything more disgusting than these macho men who come home to their little bitches and broods of squawking brats with nothing more on their minds than a good steak, a good beer and a good b.b.bed?

I'll say it again. Destroy masculinity. Twist it. Get the men to dress up in women's clothing if you can. Convince them that they *are* women—make them take hormones and wear a wig and get false breasts and have an operation to cut off their horrible genitalia. Get them into wild, raving drug-induced sodomy. D.d.drag them down. Degrade them, humiliate them and then make them think they're having fun and "being themselves."

D.d.destroy masculinity. I hate it. I hate it because it was the form that *he* took. Imagine the Enemy lowering himself to become one of the b.b.bearded, smelly, sweaty, long-haired half-breeds! He deserved to die in pain for assuming such a disgusting disguise.

We hate it! We hate it, slugs and worms! It burns us! This man burns us! He hurts our eyes. He tricked us! He tricked us by becoming a man; so destroy them! Destroy the men. They are horrible. Destroy them, I say! Destroy them!

A sharp report as a firecracker then the sound of sizzling, hissing and screaming.

Slugs! Worms, I've erupted. Aaargh! I'm melting! Grimwort, help. Help! Stop laughing! It's not f.f.funny! It's not funny, I say! No, don't send for the Flanks! I'll be alright in a moment.

A bell clangs. A siren wails. Doors slam and voices rumble as the class changes.

DAY TWENTY-EIGHT ~ *Monday,* Fourth Week of Lent

Chamber 101

Slubgrip's voice:

Now then, worms, I hope you haven't found that diversion into the messy business of marriage to be too tiresome. It's time to get back to the philosophical foundations of the popular culture we've created. A bit of concentration in this area pays great dividends later.

If you concentrate, you might even end up with a glittering career like Grimwort there, and after centuries of hard slogging ascend to the heights of becoming an assistant professor. What do you think, Grimwort, my old toad? Isn't it just the most wonderful thing to fetch lava for someone, stay up till all hours grading papers and prodding sleeping slugs?

Snickers and guffaws.

Poor Grimwort. He's an example of mediocrity being mistaken for seriousness.

I've explained how we get relativism and materialism into every aspect of culture. With that comes the sort of atheism we like: atheism by default. Once you get the humans to believe there is no such thing as truth, it's only a short jump for them to accept that there's no grandaddy up in the sky who is the source of truth.

Once relativism is in place as the foundation, consider the implications for the right understanding of history. First you must understand the prevailing view as it has been communicated by the Jews and Christians. That nauseating book of fairy tales they call the Old Testament creates the impression that there is some sort of magnificent meaning to history.

It gives the impression that there is what our academic agents call a "metanarrative". This is the bizarre idea that the Enemy is like a playwright in the sky who is composing some great drama. They think this "great story" gives meaning to the whole spread of history, as if the Enemy had some sort of master plan for the universe.

Happily we've been able to undermine this foolishness. To help your patient see what a farce it is, just prompt him to ask a few questions. "Why should the Jewish people be special? Why not some other nomadic tribe or some other race or civilization?" Get him to ask, "Why on earth should the rabbi from Nazareth be 'the One' and not some other prophet from some other tribe?" Make him wonder why that particular religion should be the 'right' religion and all the others wrong.

Thanks to Our Father Below and many years of hard work, the truth can be told at last. Jesus Christ was just another wandering, wild-eyed Jewish apocalyptic preacher. He suffered from a religious mania like so many slightly insane humans. He did not found a church. It was put together by his obsessed followers, and they happened to hit it lucky three hundred years later when the emperor decided to become a Christian.

Not only have we eroded the idea that the rabbi's pathetic tale is the meaning of history, but we've succeeded in showing the hairless apes that there is no overarching meaning to history at all.

Grimwort, it looks like Slurge has dozed off again. Take that prod and give him a short, sharp shock will you?

A yelp.

Welcome to the world of the living, Slurge. If you fall asleep again, I'll have you in the chokey for a few days.

Where was I? Oh yes. "Historicism" is the name of this philosophy. Write it down, worms. Historicism is the idea that there is no great story of salvation. There is no greater meaning because there is no great storyteller in the sky to give it meaning. Consequently, history is simply the random gathering of events that motivate other events. Kingdoms rise and fall. Great men struggle for power. So what? There are wars. People die. Some people get rich. Then they die. Some people are poor. Then they die. Life goes on. That's it. Get over it.

What this means, very simply, is that history doesn't matter. What matters is who is winning or losing and what your man has to do to get ahead. Not only does history not matter, but tradition does not matter. Tell him that anything from the past is dead. He should throw it away.

Furthermore, not only does tradition not matter, but you must get your patient to see that what does matter is that he adapts as quickly as possible to the demands of this present moment. If there is no meta-narrative or great tradition which might challenge the prevailing culture, then there is no greater belief system to which your patient should conform.

The simple elegance of the theory is breathtaking. The implications are especially pleasing. You see, worms, if there is no overarching meaning to it all, then neither is there meaning to each individual human life. Your patient will find this disconcerting at first, because the naked baboons all like to think they are important. But once he accepts the truth, you'll find that your tempting will be far easier because once he sees that his life has no ultimate meaning, he'll soon realize that it doesn't matter what he does.

That's all. Weave historicism into your patient's worldview. Let it be the underlying foundation to articles, TV shows, movies and academic work. This foundational lie will do more to promote our cause than most any other because it lies hidden and is rarely even spoken about. It is an assumed position, and it is all the more powerful for being an *underlying* assumption. We like that, worms. There's something pleasing about using camouflage and lying hidden in the grass waiting to strike.

A bell clangs.

There's the bell. Be gone.

DAY TWENTY-NINE ~ *Tuesday,* Fourth Week of Lent

Chamber 101

Slubgrip's voice:

You'll forgive me, slugs, for being delighted with today's subject, but it really is one of the most brilliant and useful tools we have for establishing the kind of popular culture we need for successful tempting.

It's called progressivism. Write it down parasites. Historicism says, "History is bunk." If history is bunk, then the only thing that really matters is what's happening now. Progressivism takes it a step further and assumes therefore that this moment is better than anything that has gone before.

Progressivism is a logical consequence of Darwinism. Darwin proposed the idea of the survival of the fittest and the gradual evolution of species. This brought about an understanding of human history as a long gradual ascent from the primordial mud to the zenith of modern man. We therefore get the humans to assume that humanity must be marching relentlessly upward, and every age is automatically getting better and better.

The idea that the human beings are at the zenith of their development is illustrated by their meteoric development of technology. How can he resist? How can it not be true that he is getting better and better? He has gone from the cave to the computer, from baboon to landing on the moon.

Progressivism is one of the Father Below's ideas I find most pleasing because it becomes an infallible doctrine of the modern humans. Furthermore, they can't help thinking that this great ascent of man is not just random chance, but that they are the proud agents of that change. Make them feel that the progress is *their* progress. They have taken charge of the future. Get them to feel personal pride at such a brave, new world that has such iPhones in it!

One of the most laughable examples of their naivety in this regard is the twentieth century. By good luck and hard work, we were able to have not one, but two world wars. In addition we had the triumph of Soviet Russia, the Chinese Revolution, two atomic bombs and umpteen other wars, dictatorships and revolutions. In the twentieth century we accomplished more bloodshed, genocide, terror, torture, death and destruction than the world had ever seen, and yet modern humans continue their starry-eyed belief that they are the most advanced and progressive humans ever to walk the earth. It's delightful, isn't it, worms?

A natural consequence of progressivism is the automatic assumption that everything old is bad and everything new is good. If we want an idea to be accepted, we only have to tell them that it is a new idea.

We have used this idea very nicely within the Christian churches. In a mad rush to make their message relevant, they've thrown out everything old and seemingly unbelievable. We've gotten them to dismiss the Bible stories with miracles for modern, relevant interpretations. Even better, we've gotten them to abandon historic Christian doctrines and exchange "traditional morality" for "new expressions of human sexuality."

Should the hidebound and narrow-minded Christians balk at same-sex marriage, re-marriage after divorce, or abortion, the progressives remind them that "the Holy Spirit blows where he will, and he is always leading the Church into new and exciting paths." "Be open to the Spirit!" our progressive Christians cry.

With very little effort, you can get your religious progressive to develop a nice-self righteous tone. Get him to play the wounded victim when he is challenged. Make him expect persecution for his radical views, and when that persecution comes make him into a martyr for the progressive cause.

There is nothing more satisfying than to get a progressive Christian to abandon every tenet of Christian belief and embrace moral views completely contrary to their religion while believing themselves to be the only truly authentic Christians.

A bell clangs.

Slime along, slugs. There's the bell.

DAY THIRTY ~ *Wednesday,* Fourth Week of Lent

Chamber 101

Slubgrip's voice is heard:

Worms! Do try to engage those minuscule organs you call brains! There is much to discuss today, and I fear it may be beyond you.

Allow me to summarize: Our control of popular culture is rooted in Our Father Below's brilliant observation that there is no such thing as truth. Our job is to integrate this basic assumption into society at every level.

Once the hairless apes have accepted that there is no other reality than what their physical senses verify, several other consequences arise that help move our plans forward. Historicism teaches them that there is no meaning to history, and with progressivism they are fooled into thinking that in each and every way in each and every day they are getting better and better.

This unremitting pessimism about the past and optimism about the future can be combined very neatly to bring about a more aggressive part of our plan: to get the humans to make the world a better place.

That is, what *we* consider a better place. You see, when the creatures stop believing in the reality of another world, they invest everything in this world. Once they are convinced that they are on a constant upward ascent, they will make it their purpose to facilitate this irresistible ascent.

They will conclude that the only way to make the world better is to make as many people happy as possible—to bring about the greatest good for the greatest number. This is what we call utilitarianism.

Show your patient that the greatest good for the greatest number is an eminently practical creed. If something promises to provide happiness for a large number of people it must be "good." Therefore, what is cheapest is best. What is most cost-effective is best. What gives the most instant pleasure is best. What gets the job done is best.

Utilitarian decisions are made by nameless businessmen and bureaucrats according to the demands of their budgets, statistics and market surveys. They will be so blinded by their enthusiasm and practical good sense that they will not see the immense pain and suffering their shallow philosophy brings about.

Let me give you an example: Let us say that one of your clients works as a manager in a large corporation. His bosses have told him that the business is going through a financial crisis. We have made him believe that efficiency and the bottom line are all that matters. He will therefore look for the quickest and easiest way to make the greatest savings in order to save his own skin.

His belief in practicality and the bottom line will blind him to any creative and positive solution to his problem. Instead he will simply fire people. He won't be concerned about their loss of livelihood, the ruined lives, the wives and children who might be made homeless. Instead he'll spout truisms about "cost effectiveness," "market forces" and "eliminating waste."

When utilitarianism is combined with politics, the results could hardly be more pleasing. If you find yourself working with a politician, utilitarianism will be one of your most useful tools. The politician is instinctively utilitarian. If it wins votes, it works. If you can get your politician to subscribe to some sort of ideology which is attached to utilitarianism, the possibilities are almost endless.

Let us say the politician wants to usher in a new order of economic equality. As a utilitarian, he wants to achieve the greatest good for the greatest number. Also as a utilitarian, he wants to do so in as efficient a way as possible. Therefore, he rounds up the rich people, takes all their stuff, chops off their heads and gives their riches to the poor. It's done. Economic equality has been achieved at the drop of a hat, and if the head is still in the hat when it drops, no great matter.

The utilitarian leader will thus wage war, murder millions, quash culture and destroy whole civilizations in an efficient attempt to make the world a better place. Furthermore, the politician really will believe that he is "serving the people" and bringing about the best world for the largest number of people while he is feathering his own nest, awarding his cronies with hefty contracts and working to make the elite even more wealthy and powerful.

The delightful thing about this, my dear fellows, is that it all follows directly from our focus on materialism. If the only world is the physical world, then the human beings have no hope of heaven or fear of hell, and if there is no heaven to win or hell to pay, then why not kill millions? If they believe that there is nothing after death—nada—zilch—zero—then killing one person or a million is no worse than pulling weeds.

The results in Auschwitz, the Gulag, the Killing Fields, the abortion clinics and Chairman Mao's China are simply too delicious for words!

Is that the time? I've enjoyed our session today. Scuttle off now to your next class, will you?

Sounds of movement as the students leave the room. Slubgrip:

Ahh, Snort? How very nice to see you again! Grimwort, get lost. I need to talk with Snort confidentially.

Now that you're ensconced in Thornblade's office, my boy, I've got a little job for you. I understand that Thornblade's secretary keeps files on the faculty and staff. In order for my little ruse to succeed, I need to have a bit more information about Snozzle. I've managed to get a key to the file room, and I was wondering if you might slip in there and make a copy of Snozzle's files for me. It won't be forgotten, Snort!

When I'm in charge, you'll get your reward.

DAY THIRTY-ONE ~ *Thursday,* Fourth Week of Lent

Chamber 101

Slubgrip's voice:

Attention worms, annelids, slugs and grubs. Quiet! Does Grimwort need to use the prod to bring some order out of chaos?

A loud zap and a yelp is heard.

Ahh. Grilled escargot is on the menu boys.

Giggles. guffaws and growls

Now then, we have seen how, once relativism is established as a foundation for the humans, it soon influences everything else. The result is very pleasing.

If there is no objective truth, then there is no objective reality other than the physical world. If there is no other spiritual realm, then there is no heaven, no hell, no afterlife and no God. The pleasing thing about Our Father's philosophy is that millions live according to this creed of relativism, but very few would call themselves atheists.

Therefore what we have established in the developed world is a kind of practical atheism. In the old communist regimes, atheism was a state-imposed doctrine. In the developed countries it doesn't need to be. The people follow our belief system very happily. They are utilitarian, relativistic, materialistic atheists through and through without knowing it.

The delightful irony is that many of them go to church on Sunday. Because the practice of their religion is individualistic, sentimental and utilitarian, it has become one more useful weapon in our arsenal. You see, dear slugs, their beliefs and moral practices are no longer decided by some authoritative book or church; they decide their own beliefs and morals according to their feelings or what seems practical to them.They say they believe in God, but it is a god of their own making.

This new religion is so much better. The followers of the "old time religion" were always rattling on about "a great battle between heaven and hell." The preachers roared in horrible terms about the "saving blood of the Lamb" and the need to "save souls." Catholic priests spoke about the fear of hell and the hope of heaven. The old religion was an unfortunate blend of saints, supernatural realities and sacraments of salvation. They were all quite obnoxious back then, teaching their children to avoid sin and to be aware of the temptations of "the world, the flesh and the devil."

Happily all that is gone. Now Christian preachers are more likely to talk about how to manage your money, raise well-scrubbed teens and build self-esteem. They avoid all talk of sin and damnation in favor of lessons in self-help, positive thinking and the assurance that they are all going to a happy heaven when they die, because after all, they are all such wonderful people.

Catholics have forgotten those gloomy old confessionals and grotesque Gothic churches and now worship in large warehouses or carpeted churches that look like teepees or ice cream cones that have fallen upside down. The people wander into church in shorts and flip-flops while their pastors are on a par with the Protestants—preaching about being nice to everyone while the praise band leads sentimental ditties about gathering together to make the world a better place.

American Christians are no threat to us because they are more American than Christian. Most of them are indistinguishable from their secular neighbors. The especially delightful thing about this state of affairs is that rather than Christianity being a challenge to our worldview, it has become the ultimate ally.

The graying members of the American churches have turned Christianity into a practical society for doing good and being nice, and they have been blind to the fact that without a supernatural dimension there is really no reason to have a religion at all. Their younger generation is not so stupid. It doesn't take them long to realize that they don't need to go to church to be good, nice people. They can volunteer to do community work and be tolerant, have straight teeth, good hygiene and be nice to others without getting up early on Sunday mornings to sing gloomy hymns and listen to a bad sermon by a fat hypocrite.

The atheism we have been able to achieve in the developed countries is far more brilliant than our brothers in the communist countries. In the West we have an atheistic, materialistic culture with a veneer of Christianity. Their Christianity has absorbed our philosophy, and it has done so with a smiling American cheerfulness and optimism.

The icing on the cake is that they have used their version of the Christian faith as the ultimate blessing on their materialistic worldview. In other words, our atheism has become their version of Christianity. Furthermore, they are totally unaware of what has happened and are as pleased with the result of our work as they would be on a morning in Disneyland.

We have seen very few success stories like the one in the United States, my dear worms. It is your job to help preserve the accomplishments we have made.

Next week I will outline the practicalities of communicating this message to the masses, and how we hammer home our philosophies. On Saturday Claxton will lecture you on politics, and on Sunday I have arranged for Dowdy to entertain you about journalism.

There's the bell. Off you go, slimestrings.

DAY THIRTY-TWO ~ *Friday,* Fourth Week of Lent

Slubgrip's Lair

Slubgrip's voice is heard:

Why, if it's not my dear old friends Crasston and Snozzle! What a surprise! Delighted, delighted! Come in, come in. To what do we ascribe the pleasure of your visit? Would you like to sit down? Why not have a drink? I'm taking a glass of fumes with a few tablets—nursing a terrible headache. Seems to hit me every Friday for some reason. You too? I'm so sorry.

Why not at least have a cup of lava? No? You'll remain standing? That's fine. Please suit yourselves, but you don't mind if I have a cup?

Now my dear fellows, what can I do for you? I say, is it really necessary to have half a dozen Flancks with you in uniform and with the pitchforks just to visit your old friend Slubgrip?

Crasston: Let's get straight to the point, Slubgrip. We've heard rumors about you.

Snozzle: That's right. Rumors. Nasty rumors.

Slubgrip: Really! Whatever could that be about!?

Crasston: Some people say you're unhappy.

Snozzle: That you've been causing trouble.

Slubgrip: Causing trouble? Me? I'll admit it was not to my liking to be tricked at the Master's banqueting hall, then flushed into the infernal sewers, but let bygones be bygones. It's all water under the bridge. Live and let live, I say.

Crasston: We've had some informers telling us that you and Knobswart are planning a little coup.

Snozzle: Planning to overthrow President Thornblade.

Crasston: And us.

Snozzle: Yeah. And us.

Slubgrip: *(Chuckles.)* Snozzle! Crasston! I wouldn't undermine you. I consider you to be old friends! I expect it has all been a ghastly misunderstanding. Allow me to explain.

Crasston: We don't much like your explanations. Do we, Snozzle?

Snozzle: No. We don't much like your explanations.

Slubgrip: No need to be aggressive, boys. The explanation is simplicity itself. It's like this. You see, some of the students don't happen to like my tactics...err, I mean my technique. My teaching technique. To put it honestly. They're out to get me.

Crasston: What do you mean, they're out to get you?

Slubgrip: You know how it is here below. Spies and counter spies, subterfuge, betrayals, lying and scheming all around. One of the fellows who is loyal to me—a very decent sort of demon named Snort—has been gathering information, and he says that the plot has been against me and not against you and President Thornblade.

Snozzle: What are you talking about? We have our information. We have our sources.

Slubgrip: Of course you have, my dear Snozzle. Of course you have. But can you trust them? Snort tells me that the students have been putting together a little mock rebellion against the administration, and especially against President Thornblade.

Crasston: That's right. That's what we've heard.

Snozzle: And we've heard that you're behind the whole thing.

Slubgrip: And that's exactly what they want you to think, dear fellows. I daresay I even know who your source is. It's my rather slimy and disgruntled Associate Professsor called Grimwort. Am I right? Ahh! I can see in your faces that I am indeed right!

Crasston: So what about it?

Slubgrip: Grimwort took against me because I sometimes rib him a little in class. He even said, "I'll get you, Slubgrip. You wait and see if I don't!" He threatened me openly, dear fellows! In front of the whole class!

Snozzle: What's your point, Slubgrip?

Slubgrip: My point is that Snort has informed me that Grimwort has been stirring up the students and telling them to blame me for the rebellion in order to make it seem as if I am planning a coup.

Crasston: Why would he do that?

Slubgrip: Why, to get his revenge on me, of course, and probably because he wants my job. If he can get you and the Flancks to come here and haul me off to the chokey, that will open the way for him. Think about it, my dear fellows. I've been around a long time. I know how the system works. Do you really think I would do something so amateurish and bold as to plan a coup against yourselves and President Thornblade?

It's ridiculous. I know my place. Teaching here at Bowelbages has not been my preferred assignment, I'll admit, but I wouldn't imperil my whole future and chances for promotion by rank insubordination and rebellion, now would I? Of course not.

Crasston: How do we know what you're saying is true?

Snozzle: Yeah, how do we know you're not lying?

Slubgrip: Haul Snort in and ask him. He'll not only confirm what I'm telling you, but he's got two or three friends, who are also my best students, who will tell you that Grimwort is the amateur who is plotting behind our backs. In fact, I don't have evidence for this specifically, but I wouldn't be at all surprised if Grimwort's little rebellion actually has some teeth in it. I doubt whether he would plan to overthrow President Thornblade, but he may have his eyes on one of your positions.

Has he ingratiated himself with you? Flattered you? Given you gifts? Yes, I thought so. If I were you, I would check out his stories and watch your back.

Snozzle: You think so?

Crasston: You think we shouldn't trust him?

Slubgrip: I wouldn't if I were you, but I'll tell you what, I've managed to get Snort a job in President Thornblade's office. I'll ask him to keep an extra ear and eye open when it comes to Grimwort, and we'll pass on to you whatever we discover.

We're on the same team, Crasston and Snozzle. Same team. Don't forget it!

DAY THIRTY-THREE ~ *Saturday,* Fourth Week of Lent

Chamber 101

A smooth, charming voice with a slight Southern drawl. It is the demon Claxton:

Well, how are y'all doing? My old friend Slubgrip said you were just about the brightest bunch of students he's ever had the privilege of teaching.

I felt lucky to be invited to be your guest speaker today on the subject of politics and practicality. Now, let me tell you something, fellas, if you should happen to find yourself in charge of a politician one day, you will have landed on your feet. Politicians are just about the easiest work you can get. Shucks, the fellows I've had from time to time have been so easy that I sometimes wondered who was tempting whom! I barely had an idea for some sort of skullduggery before they had already thought of it.

Of course, once in a while you do find a politician who starts out with some misguided idea that he is going to "serve the people." That doesn't last long. You can turn that one around lickety split. When he lines up with the rest of them to get his snout in the trough, all you have to do is tell him that he's taking the bribes, the pork, the kickbacks so that he can better serve the people. Tell him he's doing it for them. He's bringing jobs to the district and so forth.

The other ones who are a curiosity are the ones who still believe they have come into politics to "make the world a better place." They might seem to you to be a nuisance, but believe me, they are the best politicians of all. What you need to do is feed them some sort of ideology.

It really doesn't matter which—right-wing conservatism or left-wing communism—they're all the same as long as you make sure your man is willing to impose his ideology on others.

The trick is to make sure his ideology is half-right and half-wrong. Remember, boys, the half-truth is always more convincing than either the whole truth or a whole lie. Mix it up. If your politician is on the left, it's fine if he thinks he is helping the poor, ending poverty and bringing peace and justice to the world, but to do all that you must get him to destroy the family and the Enemy's quaint idea of "morality." Get him to vote for abortion not because he wants to kill babies, but because he wants to help women. Get him to vote for same-sex marriage not because he wants to destroy family life, but because he wants to bring about justice for gay people. Get him to vote for wealth redistribution not because he wants to rob the rich, but because he wants to help the poor. It's always a delight to get the humans to do the wrong deed for the right reason. Politicians are especially good at it.

If your man is right-wing, you play the same trick. Get him to start a war—not because he's invading another country to plunder their wealth, but because he is bringing them liberty and freedom. Get him to vote for low taxes and small government, not because he wants to make the rich richer, but because he wants to "give opportunity to the little guy." You get the idea. Set them up against each other, and never allow your politician to be in favor of both traditional morality *and* a bias for the poor. The right wing should support the rich but favor traditional morality. The left wing should support the poor and favor progressive morality.

Make sure your man always does what is practical. He needs to make decisions on a utilitarian basis. Tell him that's the best way to serve the people. Once you've set that up, it will be easy for you to get him to wage war, oppress the workers, drive the nation into debt, make corrupt deals for his cronies and do just about every form of evil under the sun.

With that philosophy in place, he will do all those things and think himself a clever politician, and when he retires, he will paint himself as an elder statesman and pretend to go around the world as a "peacekeeper" or "human rights campaigner" while all the time he's also collecting fat fees on the speakers' circuit and using his contacts to hook hefty "consultancy" fees.

Dowdy will be in tomorrow to talk to you about journalism. Good luck to you!

Dwight Longenecker

DAY THIRTY-FOUR ~ *Sunday,* Second Week of Lent

Chamber 101

The husky, weary and slurred voice of the tempter Dowdy:

Will you guys sit down and shut up! Grimwort, you know what to do.

Yelps and squeaks. A fight breaks out—crashing of furniture, snarling and growls with howls of pain.

Sit down, I say! That's better. Nothing like a few shocks from the prod to calm the boisterous. Slubgrip said I'd have to keep a close fork on you slugs. He says you're fed up, bored and unruly on Sundays.

I'm not surprised. Sunday's the worst day of the week. It's been that way for over two thousand years. None of us are quite sure why, but there's always this annoying stench that drifts down on Sundays—even down here to the lower regions. It's like someone has opened a window on an April morning. It is like radiance and fragrance combined. I hate it. It stinks, and it gives me a headache.

I'm Dowdy. I work in the papers. I have for centuries. If you're assigned to a journalist, reporter, editor or anyone else in the industry, if you remember a few tricks of the trade, your job will be a piece of cake.

First things first. You have to remind your patient who pays the bills. Newspapers, magazines, news websites, networks, television and radio— they're all owned by somebody, and that somebody writes your patient's paycheck. You got that? He who pays the piper calls the tune. Your patient might come into the job with stars in his eyes about "courageous investigative reporting." That's horse crap. Teach him to listen to what the boss wants and teach him to deliver.

Second thing for your boy to remember is that the boss has a boss. Beyond the editor is the owner of the network and beyond the owner of the network is the owner of the owner. In other words, there are other powers that want the news to say what they want it to say. Your patient should be aware that he really doesn't want to cross the big boys. If they want to push something, he should push it. If they want to kill a story, he kills it.

Third thing to remember is that the news is not about the news. It's about how you report the news. What facts do you choose to report? What stories do you pick up? The ones you ignore are usually more important than the ones you choose. Let's deal with religion for an example. Is there a story out there about some religious group that is succeeding and doing well? Forget it. Drop it. No one wants to hear stories like that.

What the readers want is the juicy stuff. Dish out as much as you can about Catholic priests molesting little boys. Don't let that one rest. Get your reporter to hound pastors and Christian leaders about financial corruption, sexual adventures or just plain eccentric habits or ideas. Paint the Enemy's people as dangerous sex offenders, lunatics and oddballs. Paint our people as the sane, happy, attractive, sensible folks next door. If one of our people messes up, drop it. If one of the Enemy's stumbles, kick it up it to the front page.

The next thing you got to remember is mood. Mood. You gotta have mood. It doesn't really matter what the facts are. Your guy or gal has got to write the story in a way that suits us. Everything the Enemy wants to communicate you cast in a shadowy, dark or doubtful way. The things Our Father Below wants to promote you tell in a bright, cheerful and upbeat way. We're talking about emotions here—heart stuff. Tell the facts, but don't tell them straight.

Finally, you have to remember that journalism is about entertainment. The pea-brained hairless apes don't want to think. They want to be entertained. Horrify them with crime and violence. Amuse them with celebrity gossip. Enrage them with injustice. Frighten them with groundless threats about the future, and confuse them with misinformation about the past. All of this is like a conjurer's sleight of hand. It's misdirection. Get them absorbed and addicted by the news you present, and they'll never be aware of what we are really accomplishing behind the scenes.

It's hard work and the Enemy does not sleep. Let me tell you, with the new technologies we're working overtime. Nowadays, who can keep up with it? Blogs, websites, texts, Twitter, Facebook, you name it. The news is out there and it's proliferating like crazy. The problem with this is that there are too many of the Enemy's agents at work. We used to control the papers, the TV and the radio. Now anybody and his mother can make a video, write a blog, publish a newsletter, a paper, a book! It's all going to pot.

I like chaos, but this is going too far. Maybe we ought to pull the plug on the whole internet thing and make it come crashing down. That'd teach them.

I'm exhausted. There's the bell. Clear off. Where's my glass of fumes? I'm exhausted.

DAY THIRTY-FIVE ~ *Monday,* Fifth Week of Lent

Chamber 101

Over the clatter of furniture and the rumble of voices, Slubgrip's voice:

Squeeze into your seats, slugs, and try to be quiet for a few moments. Grimwort, why isn't the projector turned on? I told you there were illustrations. You there, Slime, why are you late? I know slugs don't move quickly. That's no excuse. Where's the prod?

A zapping sound is heard, then a yelp. The voices are silent.

The smell! I love the smell of burnt slime in the morning...

I hope you nematodes enjoyed meeting Dowdy yesterday. She provides a good introduction to the more general topic of propaganda.

Propaganda, my dear slugs, we have defined in various ways down through the ages. It might be called "education" or "communication technology" or "human resources enhancement." Whatever we call it and however it's done, the bottom line is that propaganda is information control...otherwise known as brainwashing.

We use the various channels of popular culture to construct a set of assumptions to help them interpret the world. That set of assumptions is their lens—the eyeglasses through which they view everything.

One way way we do this is to fabricate an idealized future for them to attain. Through images, speeches, plays, entertainment, music, literature and every kind of communication, we build up in their imagination a beautiful and desirable world.

We want them to desire a utopia where there is no crime or inequality. We want them to dream of a society where men and women live together in brotherhood and peace—where there is no religion—where every child is a wanted child—where everyone has what they need and all share what they have.

Of course such utopias never exist—it was very clever of that insufferable English prig More that he cooked up the word which means both "good place" and "no place." He was right. Such a world never did exist, and we will make sure it never will.

You will find that the poor pinheads fall for the pipe dream every time. This is because they cannot face the fact that their unhappiness is their own problem. They have this delightful inclination to blame someone else for their misery, and this weakness is combined with the idea that it is someone else's job to make them happy. When we get these two faults working together, they are ready to blame everybody else and look for someone else to be their sugar daddy.

Propaganda is the means by which we feed both tendencies at the same time. We provide them with someone to blame while we also offer them a wizard who will give them instant happiness. You see, they must have both a scapegoat and a savior for the subterfuge to work.

Start the slide show, Grimwort. Here are some examples of our most successful campaigns in the past. Do you see the images of beautiful German youths straining forward to a wonderful future? There's the dream. Once they have taken the bait, they must then have someone to blame for the dream not being a reality. The enemy in this case was the Jews. You see, the swarthy, ugly Jew was the force holding back the realization of the dream, so that obstacle had to be removed with what we call the "final solution."

Next slide. Have a look at these large posters of Comrade Lenin, Chairman Mao and "Uncle Joe" Stalin. All of these men were successful hosts for some of our more accomplished tempters, and through propaganda we were able to transform them into mentors, father figures and exemplars for millions. These working-class heroes offered the dream, and the rich ruling classes stood in the path of the dream. The aristocrats were therefore eliminated.

The effect of propaganda is delightful. Millions of the poor hairless vermin will march along behind their dear leader blindly believing that they are bringing in a brave new world, while at the same time they are starving children, raping, pillaging, locking up whole populations in concentration camps, enslaving minority groups and massacring multitudes.

Through the images and manipulations of popular culture we enthrall the chimp men with a noble dream while millions are butchered. If they ever stop to notice, our servants simply say, "You can't make an omelette without breaking a few eggs." Then with a few party slogans, some inspiring images and the odd speech from the leader, everyone is back on track, marching in step down to Our Father's house below.

There's the bell, slugs. Be gone.

DAY THIRTY-SIX ~ *Tuesday,* Fifth Week of Lent

Day Thirty-Six - Tuesday, Fifth Week of Lent

Chamber 101

The voice of Slubgrip:

You are all rather docile this morning. The additives in the food must be working.

Yesterday you saw some historic examples of propaganda. In Europe and the Far East, the ministries of information have been crude but effective.

When you graduate, some of you will find yourselves assigned to the North American theater of conflict. What you will find there is the most delightful and powerful propaganda machine yet invented by any of our brothers below.

You have seen how images and messages have been communicated in the totalitarian regimes in order to inculcate an idealized worldview, while the tyrants in question have gone on to maraud, rape, pillage, destroy the poor and slaughter millions. In the so-called "Free World" the propaganda machine has been far more subtle, beautiful and effective than anywhere else in history.

In Russia and China we had parades with missiles and young people in uniforms waving flags, marching soldiers and huge posters of their dear leaders. In the United States we have something called "billboards."

The idea is to use images not only to sell products, but to sell a worldview. Remember the goal is to build up in the victims' minds the dream of a wonderful future. In the United States we call it "the American Dream." The original "dream" was of an independent and prosperous life attained through hard work, self-discipline and generosity. Forget about that. We have made sure that it now means getting everything you possibly can as soon as you can for as little as possible. You'll notice that this dream is just as unrealistic as the communist one.

Advertising is our main tool. Drape a lovely girl over the hood of a sports car and the poor chimps start drooling over it immediately. Show them a condominium overlooking a beach at sunset. Show them a scrumptious meal, beautiful clothes or jewelry; show them an impossibly tanned and handsome man with a dreamily beautiful woman in most any setting and they will buy not just a product but a dream, and it is this dream in which we are most interested.

Through this method the imbeciles will become thoroughgoing, self-centered, materialistic, hedonistic brutes. Furthermore (and this is so delightful it makes me giggle for joy), as they do so, they will assure themselves that they are simply being "good Americans." They would never imagine that their "consumerism" is another word for unquenchable greed, and because of their quaint isolationism, they will never even know, much less care, about the hordes of poor people in fields and sweatshops around the world who work for a pittance to provide them with their cheap luxuries.

In addition to the billboards advertising every kind of possession and pleasure, we have developed a very pleasing level of unthinking patriotism. If you work in that nation worms, drape the American flag over it and most of the North Americans will turn off their brains and start singing "God Bless America." While this patriotism can be an annoying virtue, it is a risk we are willing to take as long as we use it to blind them to the wrongdoing their country is engaged in. We don't want them to see their military as invading another country. Instead they are "liberating" those countries. They are not going in for cheap oil or raw materials or for economic reasons; they are "defending their vital national interests."

Once more we have a militaristic regime that oppresses the poor and allows insanely rich people to grab yet more wealth from those stricken with poverty, and on top of it they think themselves the happiest, nicest, healthiest and most wonderful people who ever walked the face of the earth. Despite the fact that they spend trillions of dollars on the most advanced weaponry and military forces, 90 percent of them would never, for a moment, consider their country to be aggressive. They never give a thought to the impact their insatiable consumption has on the world. After all, they would say, "It's just business."

Oh, my dear earthworms. What a thrill it gives me just thinking about it. I only hope you have the pleasure one day of strolling through Times Square or Picadilly Circus. These shrines to our propaganda successes are exciting to see. There the advertisements are ten stories high! The glittering lights and flashing screens pulse with pleasure! The huge images of sex and power are far, far more seductive than all the gods and goddesses of old! The images and slogans of consumption blaze across the night sky—all of it one huge, glorious and unbelievably beautiful Vanity Fair.

There, now I've gotten so excited I've spilled my cup of lava and it's burnt a hole in the desk. Grimwort, go the janitor's cupboard, will you, my good worm? Clean up the mess before you go. Chapter fifteen for homework, slugs.

Now be gone, you slimy diabolicals.

DAY THIRTY-EIGHT ~ *Wednesday*, Fifth Week of Lent

Day Thirty-Eight - Wednesday, Fifth Week of Lent

Slubgrip's Lair

A knock on a door. Footsteps. A door opens. Slubgrip's voice is heard.

Is that you, Knobby? Ah, good, good. Come in. Has anyone seen you?
Listen, my old friend, I have just gotten back from seeing Thornblade. I thought after that visit from Crasston and Snozzle that I really ought to take action, and I wanted you to know about it.

Flaunt—you know, Crasston's secretary? She gave me a copy of the file on Thornblade that she took from Crasston's office. She wasn't very happy about the idea, and I had to exert a bit of pressure to get her to cooperate. I discovered through Snort that Flaunt was using Crasston's files to get favors from a whole range of officials throughout our realms below. It seems Crasston has extended his power much further than this university. Flaunt tells me he has a network of spies and informers in virtually every department—right down to Our Father's banqueting hall.

She was using the information in Crasston's files to get what she wanted on a regular basis and has built up a nice little hoard of trinkets and bibelots in her lair. She naturally did not want me to pull the plug on her little earner, so she gave me a copy of Crasston's file on Thornblade, and here it is. I'm not going to reveal its contents. Suffice it to say that Thornblade has a secret. If everyone knew, it could put him in the down elevator at high speed.

Well, Knobby, I went to Thornblade immediately. He was very interested to see me, and we had a very cordial talk. He was full of apologies about Crasston and Snozzle's visit to my lair. He said it had all been a mistake and a misunderstanding, and that sometimes Snozzle and Crasston's enthusiasm overtakes their good judgement. Of course I was in full agreement and took the high road. "Youthful zeal...Inexperience combined with eagerness to please"—all that rot.

I went on to say, "My dear Thornblade, far be it from me to gossip about any of your staff, but I think you should know that Crasston has put together a rather comprehensive network of spies and informers. I realize that he must do so as Head of Security for the university, but were you aware that his network extends far beyond these hallowed halls? He keeps files on practically everyone. Did you know he has a file on you?"

Thornblade was incredulous and asked my source. Of course I didn't reveal Flaunt's name, but to prove my point I gave him the file. When he read it his face went a brilliant scarlet. Fumes began oozing from those large ears of his, and I could tell he was doing all he could to contain that famously volcanic temper.

I then assured him of my loyalty and devotion. Oh, Knobby, it was really quite delicious to see him suck it up. Together Thornblade and I planned the way forward. Next Friday is the big day. Thornblade is going to send the Flancks to remove Crasston at three in the afternoon. In this way I've got Thornblade to do a good bit of our work for us.

It's all coming together nicely, but it requires a slight change of plans. You and your four classes were going to march on Crasston's office. Crasston will now be taken below by Thornblade's Flancks. Thornblade has promised to make me Head of Security in Crasston's place, so I will head over there with my students while you go to Thornblade's office with the petition.

In the meantime Sturbage, Thrallspot and Zelnick can take Snozzle with the assistance of Strump and her group of Flancks who are loyal.

Here's how we get rid of Thornblade: You will read out the petition on the steps of Draco Hall, and at the end you reveal Thornblade's secret. By then the rest of us will have joined you, and Snort will lead the students to overpower Thornblade's Flancks and take him down. That leaves the vacancy of the presidency for you to assume. I will lead the acclamations for you and you simply walk into his office and take over.

I see no reason why there should be an office of both Security *and* Detention, and if you're in agreement, Knobby, I should like to take over both departments. I think it will be run far more efficiently if Security and Detention are combined, don't you?

There are a few other details to tie up. You know this fellow Snort? I don't trust him, Knobby. He's far too obsequious for my liking. Always trying to ingratiate himself with me. Furthermore, when I arrived at Thornblade's office, I spotted young Snort slipping out the side door looking rather furtive. What do you suppose he was up to? I don't like it, Knobby, so I've asked him to join your group of students storming Thornblade's office. Keep an eye on him, and after the dust settles I want you to send him to me.

Snozzle's detention center has a nice little chamber with an adjacent fully equipped kitchen and dining hall. When it's all over, we'll have a celebration, Knobby—or should I call you President Knobswart?—and Snort will be the main course—nicely roasted, I think, with a side of roasted prig, some fried broker with a tossed floozy and a bottle of red.

DAY THIRTY-NINE ~ *Thursday*, Fifth Week of Lent

Chamber 101

Slubgrip's voice is heard.

You should understand, slugs, that this course is called Popular Culture 101 because we wish to show you how every aspect of the humans' lives can be neatly twisted to our ends.

Today's topic is sports. You may remember that some eons ago, our patients were entertained with bread and circuses. This was a fairly successful attempt by some of our hosts to keep the masses satiated with blood sports in the amphitheaters so they would not turn their attention to the corruption of their society.

Unfortunately, gladiatorial games complete with dismemberment, disemboweling and torture are off the menu. For some reason the hairless bipeds have become a bit squeamish.

I'm also sorry to say that the most entertaining aspect of the old Roman games—throwing Christians to be devoured by the wild beasts— is simply not accepted. Oh, we still have a bit of fun here and there with Christians being imprisoned, tortured and beheaded, but it's not right out in the open like it used to be. It was such fun watching thousands cheer as a leopard bit off the head of some simpering Christian teenager or a grey bearded priest was mauled by a bear.

But I am getting off track. Sports. This subject is tricky, for once again, the Enemy has all the best weapons. All we can do is re-formulate what he has created. For some inexplicable reason the Enemy has created the hairless bipeds to enjoy playing games. There is very little that disgusts Our Father Below more than this strange and infuriating behavior of the Enemy. He could have created a serious and dignified species. Instead he creates these hairless vermin who like nothing better than running about chasing a ball.

I cannot understand it. Twelve grown men in short pants will chase one another around a field for two hours getting muddy and cold and then go inside all hearty and cheerful exclaiming what a good time they've had. What about this other ludicrous pastime in which a foursome will whack a little white ball across the lawn with a club trying to knock it into a distant hole in the ground?

The result of all this is most displeasing. The brutes get together in "teams." They learn to listen to one another and make disgusting acts of discipline and self-sacrifice for the sake of "the team." Furthermore, they become physically fit. They breathe in far too much fresh air.

Most disturbingly, through these games they seem to rise above themselves. They transcend their selfishness and learn how to be "heroes" and to "overcome their difficulties." It's maddening, and just like the Enemy to be sneaky. He's always trying to insinuate some "lesson" into their most ordinary activities.

Consequently, we must be on our guard at all times. Happily, through popular culture we have been able to twist their childish affection for games rather nicely. The trick is to make sure they watch sports rather than taking part in them. By shifting them from the field to the bleachers we can turn sports into entertainment.

The move from the bleachers to the sofa is only a small step, and with only a little encouragement your man will soon be an overweight sports slob, spending hours watching games on television while consuming vast amounts of beer, pretzels and ice cream. Turning a once physically fit athlete into a sofa sloth is very pleasing indeed.

All this is grist for the mill, dear slugs. The real battles are always with the hearts and minds, not just with the bodies. Our true triumph is to turn spectator sports into a huge part of the entertainment industry. Our real goal is to create a new religion. Make your patient into a devotee, a worshipper of his team. You will enjoy it when he starts wearing the team colors, making every home game an absolute priority on his schedule and becoming a fanatic for his team. Seeing him scream and swear at the ref for a bad call, jump up and down and be passionate about a ball game is most satisfying especially when he has skipped going to church and paid a huge price for a ticket in order to go to the game.

Make sure he teaches his children the new religion of sports as well. I'm afraid they will have to play the game, but make sure they don't play it for fun. Get the parents to involve them early and inculcate in the child the need to win at all costs. It is very satisfying indeed to see a father yell and swear at his seven-year-old for striking out or missing an easy shot at soccer. If possible, the parents should invest thousands in getting their children involved in sports. If they have a church affiliation, a sports tournament on the weekend will soon take priority. The children will learn that sports come first, and church doesn't matter. With a bit of skill on your part, you'll see the child develop into an ambitious and aggressive meathead who not only wants to win, but wants to beat the other guy at all costs.

Unfortunately, dear slugs, the sports themselves can be counterproductive. Just when you thought you were winning, you'll find your patient has fallen in with some nauseating group like the "Fellowship of Christian Athletes" and instead of the sport turning him into a selfish, aggressive and shallow gladiator, you will see him turning into a self-sacrificial, noble and hard-working team player.

The way it goes is up to you, dear worms. And don't forget—there is everything to play for. Remember the Father Below's favorite maxim: Eat or be eaten. Play for keeps, worms, and may the best maggot win.

DAY FORTY ~ *Friday,* Fifth Week of Lent

Chamber 101

The clang of a bell. Rumbling of voices. Slubgrip speaks.

Grimwort, where is everyone? They can't simply skip class whenever they want. Take attendance, give me the names and I'll send them to the Flancks.

We'll have to start, worms. The others can get the notes from Grimwort. Do you hear that, Grimwort, my toad? Send them the notes.

Yesterday we dealt with the intriguing subject of sports, and I was lamenting the fact that the Enemy seems to enjoy his little idea that the hairless apes should have playtime. It is just like him to lower himself and forget his dignity in such a way. I wouldn't be surprised if those in the Enemy's realm pass their time playing games together. How ridiculous.

He would have us believe that they exist in some sort of eternal "leisure." What does that mean? Do they have regular croquet matches on the celestial lawn? Do they pick up teams for Sunday afternoon touch football? I can just hear them, "Come on, teams, it's saints against the angels again..."

The other disgusting pastime he has devised for the cretins is making things. He wants them to sing, act and dance. He wants them to write poetry, plays and stories. He likes them to paint and sculpt, build buildings, write music and be "creative." It make me sick. Furthermore, he seems to have given them not only an interest in doing so, but a portion of his own tendency to go about making things all the time. It's very tiresome.

Through all this creativity he has them longing for something called "beauty." He has made them experience a surge of pleasure and delight in the most ordinary things. They will see a distant mountain, the sunrise over a city or the smile of a child and believe it to be "beautiful."

Our researchers have yet to discover what this "beauty emotion" is or where it comes from. All we can surmise is that the poor monkey men have some sort of brain circuitry that we cannot figure out. Until we do, we must try to confuse them about what beauty really is. The best way to do this is to remind them of the little phrase, "beauty is in the eye of the beholder." Which is a cute way of saying, "Every individual can decide what they think is beautiful."

Once that is established in their minds we can then put most anything forward as "art" and they can't say it's wrong or ugly because "beauty is in the eye of the beholder." In this way we can undermine all this "art" nonsense.

So far our most successful tactic has been to captivate the artists themselves. After several centuries of hard work we have gotten them to be the sole arbiters of taste, and their audience follows along, quite happy to be bullied into pretending to like art that any child can see is not only untrue, but immoral and ugly. Ever since the Romantic period, we have been telling the artists that they must be "original" for they are, after all, unique and superior souls. We have gotten them to believe that they are the visionaries, the dreamers and the courageous individuals who "march bravely on" where lesser mortals never dare to tread.

Once they believe themselves to be superior, we get them to believe that they, and not the audience, should decide what is good art and what is not. The way to boost this is to make the artist into a celebrity.

It works like this: first you take a mediocre artist. He believes that to be great he has to be original. (By this he means he has to get people's attention.) So encourage him to produce something vulgar and shocking—a head made of frozen urine or a huge pile of animal fat carved into a backside, or an unmade bed littered with used syringes and soiled sheets. Then once your client is notorious, er, I mean "famous," he will be able to pontificate about "art," and because of his celebrity, he can speak most any kind of nonsense and the crowds will swallow it. Most of them now will not even mention the word "beauty." Instead they talk about their political views or the "statement" they are making with their art.

Your term papers are due, slugs. Hand them in. Has anyone selected the topic "Poetry Is Profanity"? Oh, good! I look forward to reading it.

Grimwort, be a good fellow and collect up those essays, will you? And when you're done, trot down to the bog and get me another mug of lava.

Next week we're focusing on popular culture and theology. Saturday your guest speaker will be the eminent theological tempter Oskar Fullman, and Starfox will be here on Sunday with her thoughts on New Age theology. I'm sure you'll enjoy yourselves, slugs, then it's back to the grind with me on Monday, I'm afraid.

DAY FORTY-ONE ~ *Saturday*, Fifth Week of Lent

Chamber 101

A demon with a high-pitched, strong German accent is heard.

Students. It is necessary to be quiet so that I can begin my lecture. Professor Slubgrip perhaps has mentioned my name to you? I am Oskar Fullmann. As you know, I am Professor of New Testament criticism here at Bowelbages and also a specialist in Northern European theological temptation systems.

Although our research has been focused on the area of academic theologians, our influence has been much wider. Every man and woman preparing to be a Christian minister has had to study theology. Every person engaged in biblical studies or planning to do church work of any kind has been exposed to our work. Although our focus is narrow, our reach is wide.

To understand theological temptation systems, you must grasp one simple principle. It is our goal to help Christian students understand that the ancient worldview of the biblical peoples is no longer applicable to modern human beings. Allow me to explain. The ancient worldview is of a three-level universe. There is the earthly plane, the heavenly plane and the underworld. Simple, superstitious people believed that God lived above the clouds with the angels and saints, and demons lived underground where hell existed. Modern people have discovered that there is no heaven on the other side of the clouds and the underworld is no more than cave systems and volcanos.

Therefore we make it clear that the whole cosmic system of angels, demons, heaven and hell is mythological. The beliefs that go along with this mythological system are no more than make-believe. Stories of miraculous healing, a virgin birth, exorcism, resurrection and ascension are all mythological. Our work has been to help theologians construct a new belief system that retains the moral teachings of the rabbi from Nazareth while reinterpreting the mythological elements in a way that is acceptable to modern men and women.

With a bit of thought you will see how brilliant our work has been. First of all, it is very unlikely that all ancient people believed that God was on the other side of the clouds and demons lived underground. However, it suits our purposes to say they did. There is also no evidence that human beings dismiss the supernatural simply because they are living in the modern age. The persistence of religion proves that billions of the hairless chimpanzees do, in fact, believe in a supernatural realm.

However, by saying that modern people do not believe in these things, we immediately establish the value system that for a human being to be considered modern and well-educated, he cannot possibly believe in the supernatural.

Furthermore, the work of the theological temptation experts has an even more pleasant result. We have now had several generations of theologians who do not believe any of the core doctrines of Christianity, but they continue to practice as ordained clergy through the trick of "de-mythologizing" or "re-interpreting the Scriptures."

So we may have an Protestant pastor who does not believe the resurrection is possible, but he stands up on Easter day to say, "We rejoice in the power of the resurrection. Alleluia!" You see? He uses the traditional language, but what he means by this language is, "In some way we would like to believe that the beautiful teachings of the rabbi continued to be admired and taught by his followers even after his tragic death. In this way the rabbi continues to live today."

It should be clear to you that the possibilities for this exquisite form of deception are endless. An Episcopalian pastor may preach about the virgin birth. His people think he believes that the rabbi was conceived supernaturally in the womb of that insufferable girl...(I cannot bring myself to speak her name)...when in fact what he really means is that the girl from Nazareth was a very nice young woman who got pregnant by mistake but faced the pregnancy with courage and love.

A Catholic priest in our grip may preach about the "real presence of Jesus Christ in the Eucharist," but he doesn't believe the bread and wine are transformed into the body and blood of the rabbi. What he means is that "in some mysterious way the Spirit of Jesus is with us when we come to Mass."

All of this is driven by the basic premise that it is impossible for modern people to believe in the supernatural. As usual, this is never communicated to ordinary people in a straightforward manner. Instead, it is your job, working in the area of popular culture, to get this idea across in a hidden way. It is never stated. It is simply assumed.

The power of this approach is really very impressive, and the work of our tempters in this area over the last century has done more to advance Our Father Below's ultimate strategy than anything else in history.

I hope I may be forgiven for having some small amount of pride in the results of our work. Now then, students. Do you have any questions?

PASSION WEEK, DAY FORTY-TWO ~ *Palm Sunday*

Chamber 101

A soft, mellow, soothing female voice is heard.

Students, may I have your attention, please? Thank you so much. Thank you.

Professor Slubgrip has very kindly invited me to speak with you today on the subject of New Age theology. My name is Margery Starfox, and I am the Director of the Institute for Occult Science. Our department has enjoyed a huge surge in popularity over the last few decades, and I would like to share with you how our work interfaces with popular culture.

First, I would like to put our discipline in a wider cultural context. You will have studied eclecticism, I believe? Yes, that's right. It's a bit like syncretism. Syncretism is the assimilation of all belief systems into one all-embracing religion. Eclecticism is more of an individual pick- and-choose belief system.

This openness to new ideas, combined with a lack of imagination and innovation among the established Christian religions, has created an opening for the human beings to explore philosophies and religious practices that are at once new and ancient.

My department works with you to promote what was once called witchcraft. We have been successful in re-imaging this concept with modern people through five tactics. The first was to dismiss the old image of the witch as a broom-flying malevolent female as a silly Halloween joke. The witch with the broom, the cackle and the green skin has become a figure of fun—a mock villain who is no more than a harmless fairy tale character.

The second task was to manage the image of the witch in a positive way. So through attractive books and movies, we shift the witch from being a villain to a misunderstood victim, or even a mysterious, powerful and positive character.

We have also engineered the images of real witches. It is no longer called "witchcraft" but "Wicca." The practitioners are good at public relations. They explain how they are "white witches" who help people to find healing and be in contact with their departed loved ones. We have promoted a friendly face for astrology, fortune-telling, necromancy, and witchcraft. Astrology and fortune-telling have become forms of counseling. Necromancy is no longer associated with creepy seances. Instead it has become "past life encounters." Demon possession we call "channeling," and witchcraft has become just "the craft."

Fourth, we have been successful in working with many different elements of the ecology movement to promote the ancient earth religion. Intellectuals write about the earth being a single organism called "Gaia," while ecology activists celebrate the spirit of the whale, the spirit of trees and the spirits of the various stars and planets. At a more mundane level, our activists are involved politically to enshrine within the ecology movement a new reverence for nature, which eventually can become a form of nature worship—old fashioned animism with a fresh face.

Finally, we have worked hard to integrate the ancient craft into modern expressions of Christianity. Feminist theologians have been led to question, and finally reject, the intrinsic patriarchy of the Judeo-Christian tradition. The rejection of patriarchy has been aligned with the movement for the ordination of women, and their embrace of an equally matriarchal belief system.

We've snapped an ecological element on to this, therefore weaving together what is essentially the old matriarchal, earth magic paganism—otherwise known as witchcraft. It lifts my heart to see wimmin priests in what were traditional Christian denominations preaching a form of Christianity in their churches while exploring and practicing witchcraft on the side.

Perhaps our most successful transition has been in the use of our traditional teachings. The sole creed of witchcraft is "Do what you will." You will recognize this as Our Father Below's creed. We have made it more palatable by adding an extra phrase. The statement now reads, "Do what you will, but harm no one."

This has helped enormously because this creed of ours is, in fact, the default creed of most modern men and women. They don't wish to follow any particular religion. They want to be left alone to do what they will, while supposedly harming no one. Most of them would not be interested in the practice of witchcraft, but when they hear our creed "Do what you will, but harm no one," they recognize it instantly as their own.

Your work is to help popularize this creed. It doesn't matter to us one bit if the humans want to practice witchcraft. In fact, it is better that most of them don't. If they started to get into witchcraft and realized that they were being led into worshipping us, and eventually opening themselves to be infested by us, they would run in the other direction. Much better, therefore, to allow them to live ordinary, selfish lives...following our creed of doing what they will while never realizing that it is our creed.

By this route we will bring many to Our Father's banqueting hall below. They may not be particularly tasty morsels, but we need quantity as well as quality.

The Fathers below are, after all, not only vicious, but voracious.

DAY FORTY-THREE ~ *Monday* of Holy Week

Chamber 101

Slubgrip's voice is heard.

This week, slugs, we will be teaching you how to deal with that monstrous fraud—the rabbi of Nazareth. You don't need me to tell you how much damage his life, combined with the efforts of a few shrewd public relations experts, has done to our cause.

The whole episode was an example of the underhanded tactics of the Enemy. We thought he was safely in his own realm, and that he had pretty much thrown in the towel and handed earth over to Our Father. Of course, we knew he kept trying to communicate with those filthy nomads the Jews, but when he appeared as one of them, we were unsure what to do. It was, of course, a triumph of Our Father Below to have the impostor killed in public, but when his body disappeared it was a twist our Father Below had not anticipated.

Of course, the rumor that he rose from the dead is ridiculous. I will explain how to do away with it later this week, but first we need to deal with the other aspects of the wandering rabbi's fairy tale, and the first to dismantle is the story of his birth.

Happily, there are so many supernatural elements to this part of the story that it is a relatively easy business to get the human beings to regard the whole thing as a pious fable. What you must do is compare the miraculous elements in the gospel story to similarly fantastic elements in myths and folk tales. Take the story of the angel Gabriel appearing to impregnate the stupid peasant girl. Tell your patient that this is not so very different from the fairy godmother appearing to Cinderella and giving her a new dress to meet the handsome prince.

Angels appearing to shepherds? Wise men following a magical star? A little cuddly baby in the manger? An ox and an ass who adore? Add more sappy elements to the story if you can: "The Little Drummer Boy," "O Little Town of Bethlehem," *The Littlest Angel*...whatever. The idea is to play up the magical, fairy tale elements of the story as much as possible. That way the half-breeds will go on believing the whole sweet story, but they will never take it seriously. It will become the stuff of children's Christmas plays, picture books and sentimental tripe.

Then take the whole charade one step further. Santa Claus. Yes, yes, I realize that "Santa" is an anagram of "Satan"—that's very clever of you, Slurge. The point here is to push our alternative myth. This involves all the Christmas extras that we've developed over the years: Santa and his reindeer, "the Night Before Christmas" and presents, Frosty the Snowman and schmaltzy Christmas carols about city sidewalks and holiday smiles all help to distract them from the real story. Throw in a hefty bit of materialistic shopping, and we will have completely separated Christmas from the horrible event in Bethlehem two thousand years ago.

What you want to avoid is any serious consideration that the Enemy was born here and what it means. Don't let your patient see that the girl risked her own life to have the child or that the father risked his reputation to take her in. Don't let him consider that Joseph and Mary were poor, working-class people. Don't let him see that they were part of an oppressed ethnic minority. Keep him away from the fact that the child's life was in danger from the beginning and that he and his parents fled from their own land as refugees. All these facts lend a gritty authenticity to the story, which is counter-productive.

If your patient starts to get interested in the actual conjunction of planets and constellations which were studied by Eastern sages, tell him the story is no more real than Pinocchio singing, "When You Wish Upon a Star." If he picks up a book (and there are too many of these) in which people give witness to their real encounters with angels, tell him the book was written by a crackpot religious woman. Should he explore the time period and investigate the historical background of the nativity story, remind him that the whole thing is a fairy tale and it would be just as sensible to go on a quest for the historical Peter Pan.

It is possible these days to get your patient to think that Jesus Christ never existed at all. Get him to read atheist websites. We've managed to create a wonderful mix of ignorance, arrogance, conspiracy theories and sophomoric arguments. They will appeal to a surprising number of your clients. If, however, he does believe that the impostor really existed, make sure that he never hears the word "incarnation." If he comes across it, dismiss it from his mind immediately. If he comes to understand what the word means, then tell him how preposterous it is that anyone would suggest that God Almighty would become a squawking, breast-sucking, defecating brat.

Tell him that the God-Man stuff was made up by later Christians who wanted to keep aspects of their pagan religion. If he starts to believe in the incarnation of the Son of God, then almost every other aspect of what our enemies call "traditional Christianity" will follow. That's why your method for dealing with the Christmas story is very important. Undermine the whole fairy tale from the start. If you can get him to see the Christmas story as make-believe, he'll soon regard the rest of the religion as nothing more than a useful fiction.

Tomorrow we'll tell you how to deal with the impostor's teachings.

By the way, you may feel some interference in the atmosphere. This week is what they celebrate as "Holy Week." They'll all be especially fervent and "prayerful." It makes me sick, and I expect some of you may well come down with something. I am usually nauseous for the entire week. Get over it, and remember the migraine you experience this week is nothing compared to the splitting, head-crushing torture that awaits you below.

DAY FORTY-FOUR ~ *Tuesday* of Holy Week

Chamber 101

A roar of voices in discussion and disagreement. The voice of Slubgrip:

I hear your rumblings and grumblings. I know you are unhappy with conditions here at Bowelbages, and to tell you the truth, I am sympathetic. Before Snort was called to serve in President Thornblade's office, he and I had a meeting. He said there was increasing discontent among the students and that an uprising was brewing.

In fact, you are not the only ones. Large numbers of faculty and staff are also discontented. We share your unhappiness at the crowded conditions, the filthy environment, the lack of proper sanitation and the heat. We are fed up with working nonstop with no break on weekends and no holidays.

We know how you students chafe under the rules from the Department of Detention. Commissioners Crasston and Snozzle are incompetent imbeciles. They may know how to run a police department, but they're ham-fisted when it comes to handling cultured and experienced demons like myself.

To be honest, slugs, I think you deserve better. I can inform you that this Saturday something will happen. "Watch and be prepared" is all I can say.

Now let's get on with the work at hand. This week we are dealing with the impostor from Nazareth. Yesterday, I explained how to deal with his birth, today we consider how to deal with his teachings.

The best method is to pick and choose. Taken out of context and cut down to size, some of his teachings can be used. Others need to be edited, still others ignored.

Here is an example. There is a story of a woman taken in adultery, and the religious leaders bring her to the man from Nazareth for judgment. The woman is to be stoned to death. The rabbi is silent, then he says, "Let he who is without sin cast the first stone." You have to admire his wit. The religious leaders slink off home, and he says to the woman, "Neither do I condemn you. Go and sin no more." What you do with this passage is portray the rabbi as a nonjudgmental, tolerant person who stands up to the judgmental, religious, self-righteous types. The way to do this is to stress his words "neither do I condemn you" but quietly forget the "go and sin no more" part.

A good many of his teachings can be used in this way. Another favorite is "Judge not that you be not judged." The way to twist this is to get your patient to resist any form of judgment on his actions. If you are clever, your patient will continue to judge others, but never judge himself. If anyone tries to call him on his selfish behavior, he plays the "Don't judge!" card. In this way, you can neatly reverse the rabbi's teachings while getting your patient to believe he is following them.

When it comes to his other teachings and actions, you must try to take from them a point or a moral that seems right, but that sidesteps what he really meant. Take his cute little story of the "Good" Samaritan. A traveler falls among thieves. The religious people pass him by, while the despised foreigner goes out of his way to assist him. This is a story about religious hypocrisy, and it is the rabbi's answer to the question, "Who is my neighbor?" You don't want to go there. Shift the emphasis and give the story an anodyne moral: "We should all be like the Good Samaritan and try to help people more."

Focus on teachings about being nice, tolerant, nonjudgmental people. Avoid all those teachings about hell, sin and punishment. Encourage sentimental stories, like the one where he takes children in his lap and blesses them, or the one where the Good Shepherd goes out into the wilderness to find the little lost lamb to bring him home. Avoid the stories where he calls people sinners, serpents or "Sons of Satan." The whole enterprise is an attempt to edit the gospels to portray the rabbi from Nazareth as a simpering, sentimental, naive and effeminate fool.

Most of all, you want to avoid the teachings where he reveals who he really is. When he says, "I am the Good Shepherd," don't let people know that he is portraying himself as fulfilling an Old Testament prophecy that God would come and be the shepherd of his people Israel. Block out those times when he calls himself "the Bread of Heaven" or "the Way, the Truth and the Life." When he says "I AM" he is using the Jewish sacred name for the Enemy himself. Explain it away. Ignore it. Strike it from the record. Pretend he never said it.

The final object when dealing with the teachings of the impostor is to portray him as no more than a good teacher who was a martyr for his cause. Compare him to other religious teachers and martyrs. Compare him to the Buddha, to Gandhi or to Martin Luther King Jr.

If he is no more than a wandering holy man, a guru or even an activist with a spiritual dimension, we can deal with him. What we don't want is this outrageous talk of him being the Enemy incarnate.

A bell clangs.

DAY FORTY-FIVE ~ *Wednesday* of Holy Week

Chamber 101

Slubgrip's voice:

Slugs, I must ask you to take what I said yesterday about a student uprising with a pinch of salt. While I am in sympathy with your grievances, do not suppose that I wish in any way to be a leader of such a student revolt. This is for you and your peers to undertake.

Today we must consider what to do with the rabbi of Nazareth's so-called "miracles." The first way to deal with these exaggerated stories is to dismiss them. One of our most successful cases was a philosopher called David Hume who simply said miracles are impossible, therefore they never happened.

The miracles can be divided into four categories. The first are the healing miracles. These are easily disposed of. What seemed like a miraculous healing was no more than the work of hypnosis upon a suggestible client.

Exorcisms? Explain away any mention of how we infest the humans. Insist that the afflicted person was mentally ill or suffered from epilepsy. Admit that the rabbi may have had some sort of healing psychic gift--— it is not unknown, but one does not have to admit of any supernatural origin. When it comes to other, more inexplicable "healings" like a blind person receiving sight, or stories of Jesus raising from the dead, point out that these stories have a special theological significance. Receiving sight is a metaphor for spiritual enlightenment. Being brought to life is a metaphor for being re-born spiritually. Obviously these stories were first told as parables, and they evolved into stories that "really happened."

The third category of miracles attributed to the rabbi from Nazareth are provision miracles. These are stories where he supposedly turned water into wine or multiplied bread and fish to feed people, or where there was a miraculous catch of fish. Use a combined argument here. First, state that these miracles are impossible and therefore there must be another explanation. The explanation is that these stories carry a theological meaning. Like the healing miracles, they were first told as parables to illustrate the theological truth, and later they came to be told as real events. They never happened in a literal sense.

Finally, we must consider what are called "nature" miracles. They say he walked on the water and calmed the storm. Point out that these stories seem to "fulfill" Old Testament prophecies. In the book of Job, our Enemy is one whose "footsteps are on the waves of the sea," and his calming of the storm is a reference making him equal to the creator God. This is obvious nonsense invented later to try to boost the claims to divinity that were being made for the loser of a rabbi. They're fiction—fabricated long after the rabbi lived and died to make him seem like the Son of God.

The point of the whole exercise is to ensure that the rabbi from Nazareth is seen as no more than an ordinary human being. Happily, much of our work is now being done for us in this area by the Christian clergy themselves. In seminary they learned from the men trained by Oskar Fullmann and his department, and now they go full-tilt preaching sermons that cleverly explain away the miracles and turn them into anodyne stories with a bland theological or moral point. My favorite example is the old warhorse of telling the faithful that the "real miracle" in the feeding of the five thousand was that everyone shared their lunch.

The excellent implications of this work on miracles is that the Christians not only don't believe in the miracles of the New Testament, but they also do not believe in the possibility of miracles in their own lives. Once we have successfully stripped the gospels of the miraculous element, it is an easy business to strip miracles out of everything.

Consequently, Christians who used to believe in the power of prayer, the Christian healing ministry, exorcism and the miracle of "living by faith" have tossed all that out the window. The modern Christian does not expect any sort of miraculous intervention in his life, and those who once believed in the supernatural efficacy of the sacraments now dismiss such a possibility with a cheerful idea that the Mass is all about "sharing the family meal." They've replaced the supernatural interaction with the Enemy with a bland religion of being nice and respectable, and the ones they are most convinced are nice, respectable people are themselves.

I don't know about you, but I am feeling rather nauseous today. It often happens at this time of the year. A certain malaise sets in—an insecurity and fear that I dislike very much and cannot explain. I think I will take the rest of the day off and go lie down.

Same time tomorrow, slugs.

DAY FORTY-SIX ~ *Holy Thursday*

Chamber 101

The voice of Slubgrip:

Worms. I am not feeling well. I had a bad night. Today's session may be shorter than usual. You can read it up in your textbooks if you wish. It's the chapter called "Mystery Solved." I need to explain, if I can, this foolishness the rabbi of Nazareth started called the Eucharist or Holy Communion.

If he could see what they have done with his simple few words at a very ordinary meal, he would be highly amused, saddened and maybe even outraged.

You will find the fullest exaggeration of this among the Catholics. They have come up with a preposterous theory that their ritual is a re-presentation of the death of the Jewish rabbi. They think by some sort of hocus pocus they are bringing his execution into the present moment. Furthermore, they believe that the bread and wine become the body and blood of the rabbi from Nazareth. Since they also believe that he is God in human form, that means that the wafer of bread and the mouthful of wine become God. If this wasn't ludicrous enough, it seems that millions of the gullible cretins really do think it is true.

The other Christians often have more common sense, but even they treat their little rituals with bread and wine with utmost seriousness. They claim that the "real presence of Jesus is there" or "we do this in remembrance of him who died for us." My point is that no matter what brand of Christian they are, they seem to believe that the bread and wine game really matters, and that somehow they are in touch with the loser from Nazareth.

What can be done about it? Trample on it, slugs. Ridicule it. Destroy it. Encourage the Christians who downplay this ritual. Find the ones who teach that it is only bread and wine and promote them. Get them to teach that the Eucharist is simply a "fellowship meal"—no more than Thanksgiving dinner. Get them to treat the Eucharist casually. Tell them it's okay to go to church in short shorts and halter tops. Get them to turn the Eucharist into a rock concert, if you can. Attack the ones who claim that it is more than bread and wine. The rabbi himself never meant for them to take his words so literally.

The worst thing about this belief of theirs is where it leads. We work as hard as we can within popular culture to cultivate a worldview in which there is no supernatural interaction between the physical world and the spiritual world. This Eucharist undermines everything we are trying to do.

They claim that through this ritual the rabbi of Nazareth is still alive and really is in touch with them. They claim that he lives in them and they live in him. What nonsense! It's impossible. It can't be possible. I refuse to admit that it could be possible.

If this were possible, then the worst imaginable scenario would develop. The Enemy would have a system whereby he has not only invaded our territory with the rabbi of Nazareth, but the perfidious rabbi is replicating himself through this grotesque ritual billions and billions of time over.

If this is true, then he has established a whole "sacramental system." It begins with baptism and faith by which the human "is baptized into Christ," and it continues through a whole lifetime of contact and interaction with the rabbi. It can't be true. If it were true, we would be outnumbered by a multitude of gruesome "Jesus clones." Then I shudder to think that even at the beginning they were called "Christians" or "little Christs."

It is grotesque. It is obscene. It is disgusting, that's what it is... disgusting!

The sound of vomiting.

Uggh. I'm sorry. I'm sick, and I can see that some of you are, too. Class dismissed. Go home. Tomorrow is the worst day of the year. I already have a splitting headache and don't know if I will get up at all tomorrow.

DAY FORTY-SEVEN ~ *Good Friday*

Chamber 101

Slubgrip's voice:

I have the most splitting headache. It feels like my head is in a vise and being slowly crushed. I see most of you feel the same. I must sit down. I can't continue standing, but I shall soldier on. Take notes if you can. I will be discussing how to deal with that gruesome event outside Jerusalem on that Friday afternoon.

What happened exactly? We know that the wandering Jewish rabbi was killed as an insurrectionist by the Roman authorities. The New Testament makes the preposterous claim that the itinerant teacher was really the "Son of God."

The fact, which we must admit, is that this really did take place. Our Father Below knew who the scum rabbi really was, and engaged him in battle from the start. He did everything he could to destroy the jumped-up hillbilly carpenter, but was prevented. You can understand Our Father's thrill, therefore, when he engineered the events that brought the wandering preacher to trial. It was touch and go. At any moment he might have slipped through Our Father's hands again. Pilate nearly released him. Herod didn't want to sentence him to death. The crowd might have called for Barabbas to be released. What delight Our Father took when he was finally sentenced to be flogged and then crucified.

But this is all that happened. The Jewish rabbi was killed. The so called "Son of God" was killed. Our Father saw that it was done. And it was good.

The maddening thing is that the whole triumph of Our Father Below has been turned around by a few fabrications, some clever theological fantasy stories and some lucky turns of events for the followers of the rabbi.

It would have been just an ordinary death of yet another rebel leader, but then there was the troublesome detail of his body disappearing. Before we knew it, his disciples were claiming that he was risen from the dead, and people believed it! They believe it still!

Then they started to speak about his death as a sacrifice. They said he was the "Lamb of God" who takes away the sins of the world. They explained that his death was a "saving action" that somehow redeemed the whole world. The claims were outrageous. How could one man's death be the action that "redeems the whole world," whatever that means?

Before we knew it, thousands were claiming to have "faith" in the rabbi. They were going through a baptism ceremony and claiming to be "born again." They claimed to have received new life through this itinerant preacher.

Worms, the only way to combat this overblown foolishness is to remind your patient what a load of complete nonsense it all is. Ask them the questions I'm asking you: "How do you imagine that one person's death saves everyone?" Ask them, "Why would the death of a criminal 'take away the sins of the world'?" Ask them, "Why does having 'faith' and being dunked in a tank of water 'join you to Christ'?" You don't even have to argue. Simply ask the questions and they will soon see just how ridiculous the whole matter really is.

The frustrating thing about all this, slugs, is that the Christian preachers have created a demand, and then they fill it. They go around telling their hearers that they are miserable sinners who need to be saved and redeemed. They keep telling everyone that they need to be forgiven and that they need a savior. Then, "Hey presto!" they pull the rabbi out of the hat, and he supplies all their needs.

Impress upon your patients, slugs, that they are just fine as they are. They don't need a savior. They don't need a redeemer. Look at us. What's wrong with us and our world?

Once you have reminded them that they don't need a savior, it will be much easier. They will be able to look at a crucifix and spit on it as we do. They will be able to laugh at all the guilty little Christians going forward to kiss the cross today, all pretending they are poor miserable sinners.

Do they want to be saved? Let them save themselves. Do they want to be free? Let them be like us. We are free, for we have made our own choices to do as we will. Do they want to be forgiven? They do not need forgiveness, for they have done nothing wrong. Slugs, get them to see that the whole sin and forgiveness thing is one big illusion from top to bottom.

They do not need a savior. They do not need a redeemer. They do not need to be forgiven. They cannot be saved. They cannot be redeemed. They cannot be forgiven. It is impossible. The events on that Friday afternoon are empty. They are meaningless.

It was nothing but the death of a petty criminal. It was the death of a loser.

I spit on it. I trample on it. I despise it. It means nothing. It means nothing. There is nothing. Nothing. Nothing. Nothing.

Moans, then howls are heard. They increase as the whole class begins howling in agony. Then the voice of Slubgrip:

My head. Oh. My head!

DAY FORTY-EIGHT ~ *Holy Saturday*

Thornblade's Office

A door opens. A deep, cultured voice is heard. It is the demon Thornblade.

Thornblade: Come in, Slubgrip. Come in. Sit down. Crasston and Snozzle, would you please step outside, and when the Flancks bring Knobswart, show him in, will you?

Snozzle: Of course, Thornblade.

Crasston: No problem, T.B.

Thornblade: Now Slubgrip, what's this we hear about you and Knobswart planning a coup?

Slubgrip: My dear Thornblade, it's all a ghastly mistake. A misunderstanding.

Thornblade: Why don't you tell me all about it?

Slubgrip: I do admit that I have been plotting a bit, but it's all relatively harmless.

Thornblade: I see. I asked Crasston and Snozzle to bring you by my office because we heard that today you were planning to lead a group of faculty and students to topple Crasston and Snozzle and even myself. The rumor was that you wished to take control of Security and Detention, and that you were going to set up Knobswart as your puppet president.

Slubgrip: Really? Why, how ludicrous! I was just in here with you last week, President Thornblade, and I assured you at that time of my undying loyalty. If I were plotting against you, I would have used what I discovered in Crasston's file against you. Instead I brought it to your attention in the proper procedure. It is true that I have no special liking for Crasston and Snozzle, and I would like nothing better than to see them gone below, but I am just a simple college teacher. Surely you don't think I have the connections to pull off a coup like that? If I may say so, I have been seriously slandered, and I am outraged.

Thornblade: Really? Then what is your version of the story?

Slubgrip: All I wanted to do was earn some points and be seen to be loyal to you. The idea was that some students would start a protest, publish a student paper, raise a petition with a few demands and just stir up a bit of rather harmless trouble. You know the sort of thing. Then I would step in to quash the student revolt, call in the Flancks, make peace with everyone and bolster my reputation as a kind but firm faculty member—one who understood the students, but most of all, was loyal to the administration.

I admit in hindsight it was rather foolish, and apt to be misunderstood. I assure you, however, that it was no more than this. Perhaps it was ill-advised. However, there were, in fact, rumblings among the students, and I thought the best way was to encourage the revolt so the true leaders would emerge so they could be put down most effectively.

My only intent in all of this was to be loyal to you and to support your presidency. These other rumors are outrageous lies.

A door opens.

Snozzle: Here's Knobswart, T.B, and here's his statement.

Thornblade: Knobswart. Have a seat there next to Slubgrip. You look somewhat the worse for wear. Have you had a bad night?

Knobswart: Bastards. They used old Stretch.

Thornblade: Yes. Old Stretch is rather trying, isn't she?

Knobswart: They didn't need to stretch me. I'd have told them everything. They only did it for fun.

Thornblade: Well, never mind. You'll recover. It's amazing how elastic most demons are. Your statement is very interesting, Knobswart. Slubgrip, it says here that you were indeed planning a takeover—that you have developed a strong following and were planning to take over Crasston and Snozzle's departments just as we thought.

Slubgrip: It's completely unfair. You know very well that one will say most anything under torture. I expect Snozzle and his Flancks cooked up the whole story, fed it to Knobswart and then tortured him to sign a prepared statement. I refuse to accept this as anything more than a plot against me. I have no idea what I've done wrong, except that I have always had enemies. No matter how hard I try, there are always people trying to bring me down. They're out to get me. Really, President Thornblade, don't believe them. Remember our conversation. Crasston is the one who is plotting against you. Don't trust them!

I admit my plot to get attention when I put down the student revolt was not the best. It was silly of me, but it was no more than that. Why not ask Snort? I told him about the plans from the beginning. He'll vouch for me.

Thornblade: That's just the thing, Slubgrip. It was Snort who first alerted us to your plans. You see, when you sent Snort over to spy on me, he told me about your idea at once and he said he didn't trust you. He then agreed to spy on you for me rather than spying on me for you. Since he told me about your plot, we have been following it all along.

Snort's information prompted me to ask Crasston to send some security men over to your classroom and your lair to install some listening devices. We've taped all your lectures and all your conversations with Knobswart and the others.

Knobswart: Then you didn't need to torture me!

Thornblade: I know. As you said, it was just for fun.

Knobswart: Bastards.

Thornblade: Crasston and Snozzle! Take Slubgrip away. Keep him in detention until we can arrange a dinner date for him in the Father's banqueting hall below.

Slubgrip: I protest! President Thornblade! This is completely unfair. I've been framed. It's not true. There's been a grave miscarriage of justice. I demand to be heard. Crasston and Snozzle are unscrupulous bullies. I can explain everything. Knobswart and I were only planning to get rid of Crasston and Snozzle. The talk about putting Knobswart in your job was my way to get Knobswart on board. I was going to make sure you were kept in power and Knobswart would be blamed for everything. I had plans. It wasn't supposed to turn out like this! Snort will tell you. He was loyal to me! You don't understand.

Knobswart: Bastard.

DAY FORTY-NINE ~ *Easter Day*

Chamber 101

The voice of President Thornblade:

Come to order, class. You are to be commended for reporting the revolting work of your Professor Slubgrip. He has been taken to detention, so I thought I would step in and take his lecture today.

As you know, today the followers of the Enemy rejoice at the so-called "resurrection." Slubgrip would have lectured you on this subject today, and Grimwort—who is taking over from him starting tomorrow—has given me his notes.

The fiction of the resurrection of Jesus Christ from the tomb was started by his first disciples after what was no more than a mistake. After his death the body of the itinerant preacher disappeared. The fact of the matter is, we are uncertain what happened to it. One of our better servants on earth—a New Testament scholar, as it happens—believes the body was left on a trash heap and eaten by dogs. That is as good an explanation as any other.

Because the body could not be located, the rabbi's followers got all excited and claimed that he had "risen from the dead." We know that Our Father Below would never have let something so stupendous take place. He engineered the impostor's death from the beginning, and he was certainly not going to allow a "resurrection" to take place.

Unfortunately, the story continued to circulate, and the followers of the rabbi became bolder and bolder. Before long, the story was believed by an increasing number of people. You know how it is: tell a big enough lie and anyone will believe it.

The lie must be exposed, and here are some tactics to do so. First of all, start with the assumption that the resurrection could not have happened simply because it could not have happened. Don't let your patient see that, by its very nature, the resurrection would be a unique event. Just insist that it couldn't happen, therefore it didn't happen.

This will leave you with a need to explain what did happen. First you can suggest that the rabbi didn't really die. This is difficult for us because we would have to admit that Our Father Below failed in his mission. Nevertheless, for a greater good it is permissible to perpetrate such a lie. Say that the rabbi survived the crucifixion, that he only swooned and went into a coma, and then he woke up later. Keep your patient at that simple level of explanation. Divert his attention, and don't allow him to ask why the professional executioners didn't follow through. Don't let him envision the whole scene, or he will ask how a man would survive such torture, wake up, roll back a three-ton stone, and step naked into a cold spring morning only to have his friends say, "He is risen from the dead!" when they would really have said, "Our friend survived his torture...let's get him to a doctor!"

All of these questions are problematic and should be avoided. It is perhaps easier to admit that the rabbi died, but that something else happened to his body. This is the view we usually take. You may suggest that the disciples stole the body, but there is the obvious difficulty that a guard was placed to prevent that, and they were not exactly the sort of dynamic characters to mount a heist. Alternatively, you can suggest that the body was thrown out and eaten by dogs, but the problem here is that it is well known that the Jews take special care in the burial of their dead—even criminals. Other possibilities are that the disciples went to the wrong tomb, or perhaps the best solution: simply claim not to know what happened.

Instead insist on what did happen. Jesus of Nazareth, the wandering rabbi, died on that Friday. He was buried. He did not rise from the dead.

It must be admitted that this is one of our weakest points. We know he did not rise from the dead, but we do not know what did happen to him. It is a problem we still have not solved. Our experts have put out every argument against the resurrection that is possible, but still the answer eludes us. Therefore the best tactic is simply to avoid the question. Do everything you can to avoid the question, and do everything possible to divert your patients from this most troublesome question.

Get them involved in any other argument but this one. Get them distracted by every other entertainment, every other passion, every other commitment, but do not let them take time to consider this matter. In fact, slugs, everything you do—all that you learn at Bowelbages University—is directed towards the avoidance of this most difficult question.

Despite the fact that this is the most monumental lie of history, the deception continues. The Enemy continues to grow his church—that pathetic family of believers in the lie of the resurrection. Year by year the lie spreads from country to country throughout this globe we call our own. Year by year the contagion spreads as more and more of the humans come to believe the lie and give themselves to the Enemy.

Somehow—in a way we have not understood—these believers share in a new kind of light and life. Something happens to them. They really do seem to connect with the wandering rabbi in some way we cannot understand.

This truth—the advance of this army of his—is terrifying to behold. Their existence is the worst outcome Our Father Below can imagine, and for his sake I hate them. I hate the miserable followers of that impostor from Galilee. I hate them all, and it is our task,my fellows, world without end, to crush them if we can.

A bell clangs.

Class dismissed.

𝔅𝔬𝔴𝔢𝔩𝔟𝔞𝔤𝔢𝔰 𝔘𝔫𝔦𝔳𝔢𝔯𝔰𝔦𝔱𝔶

Learn to Burn, Burn to Learn

◆

Memo:
From: His Eminence, Thornblade, DMn
         President and Director of Communications
         Department of Infernal Security
         Re-Education Division

To: Heads of Department - Bowelbages University

CONFIDENTIAL

Last week there was a small disturbance in our otherwise happy university family.

Professor Slubgrip, who was teaching Popular Culture 101, is no longer with us. After an unfortunate misunderstanding, Slubgrip was escorted from campus by our security services.

Slubgrip was a popular and hard-working member of our faculty, and his special gifts will be missed. However, he can be assured of our delight in his new position. We wish him a bon voyage and bon appetit.

His class will be taken by Assistant Professor Grimwort. Snozzle and Crasston will be awarded honorary Doctor of Laws at this year's commencement, and I have appointed both of them as Vice Presidents for Security and Detention.

I have appointed Snort as my personal assistant for Communications, and Professor Knobswart has been appointed Deputy Director of Maintenance in charge of Infernal Sewers and Sanitation. These appointments are effective immediately.

Thank you for your continued support.

In the service of Our Father Below.

Sincerely,
Thornblade

MORE BOOKS ~ *By Dwight Longenecker*

Fr Longenecker began writing when he joined the Catholic Church. Over the years he has written a number of books on apologetics, Benedictine spirituality and the Catholic life. Browse and purchase his books at his website: www.dwightlongenecker.com

The Gargoyle Code - If you enjoyed reading Slubgrip Instructs you should read Fr Longenecker's first diabolical instruction book *The Gargoyle Code.* In this book of Lenten Letters the demon Slubgrip tutors his junior demon Dogwart on how to tempt his Catholic patient. There is the usual skullduggery and dark humor mixed with life lessons and profound spiritual teaching. As in Slubgrip Instructs there are daily readings for every step of the way through Lent.

The Path to Rome is Fr Longenecker's first book. It is a collection of conversion stories, mostly from Anglicans. Marcus Grodi of the Coming Home Network has a chapter in the book, and Fr Longenecker's conversion story was first published here. *Path to Rome* is especially good for those who are in the Anglican or Episcopal churches, although the issues discussed are relevant to all non-Catholic Christians who want to learn more about the Catholic faith.

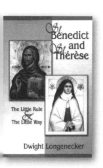

St. Benedict and St. Therese: The Little Rule and the Little Way - During his time living in England, Fr. Longenecker developed a great interest in both St. Benedict and St. Therese of Lisieux. This book studies the lives and writings of these two beloved saints. St. Benedict is like the grandfather in the family of God, and Therese is like his little grandchild. Together they complement one another and show us how to find God in the ordinary things of life.

Listen My Son: St. Benedict for Fathers - As a father of four children and a Benedictine oblate, Fr. Dwight Longenecker is ideally suited to apply the famous *Rule of St. Benedict* to family life. This book of daily readings gives the reader a portion from the *Rule of St. Benedict* for each day. After the portion from the Rule, there is a short reading that applies the timeless wisdom of St. Benedict to modern family life. This is a great gift for fathers of all ages.

Praying the Rosary for Inner Healing - God has used this book to touch thousands of lives. In a very practical and simple way, Fr. Longenecker shows how the twenty mysteries of the rosary connect with the different stages of our lives. Step by step, this book helps readers meditate on the stages of Christ's life and open the deepest areas of their lives to the healing graces of Christ.

With inspiring illustrations by Catholic artist Chris Pelicano, *Praying the Rosary for Inner Healing* has been featured on the Spirit Daily website and on Johnette Benkovic's *Living His Life Abundantly*. It gives new direction for those already used to praying the rosary and shows newcomers how to use this ancient and beautiful form of prayer in a relevant and life-changing way.

More Christianity - C.S.Lewis wrote *Mere Christianity*. Fr. Longenecker's *More Christianity* plays word games with that title and challenges Evangelical readers to move on from "mere" to "more". *More Christianity* explains the Catholic faith to non-Catholic Christians in a friendly way. It's not "We're right and you're wrong" but "What you have is good, but there is more to it than that, and the "more" is Catholicism. In this book Fr Longenecker's easy style presents a winning case for Catholicism and helps non Catholics understand what Catholics really believe.

Catholicism Pure & Simple - As the title says, this book explains the Catholic faith in a simple, clear and direct manner. Steering clear of theological jargon, churchy language, liturgical code words and pious talk, *Catholicism Pure & Simple* starts with arguments for the existence of God and moves through to the revelation of God in Jesus Christ, the coming of the Holy Spirit, the founding of the Church and the need for prayer and sacraments.

An excellent book for young people searching for the truth, this book has been used by home schoolers and confirmation candidates, as a high school and college textbook, and as a good first step for those who long for the fullness of God's truth.

Quest for the Creed - This unusual book takes the reader on a Chestertonian rollercoaster ride through the Apostle's Creed. Fr. Longenecker goes on a creative quest for truth showing that orthodox Christianity is anything but dull. Instead it is a wide-open, exciting explanation for all that was, all that is, and all that shall be.

Noted biographer Joseph Pearce has said, "In this exciting book Longenecker follows in the imaginative footsteps of Chesterton and Lewis. He sees and seizes the thrill of truth with insights of pyrotechnic brilliance. He shows us that orthodoxy is dynamic and thrilling. Hold on tight and enjoy the ride!"

The Romance of Religion - To follow Christ is to embark on the greatest adventure life has to offer. Gallivanting through the depth of stories, myths and legends, Fr. Longenecker explores the reasons to follow Christ in the great, table-turning quest that is life itself.

Drawing on movies, theology, fairy tales and popular culture, *The Romance of Religion* inspires the reader to first hear the call of Christ, then step out of his or her comfort zone to set out on the beautiful struggle.

A Sudden Certainty: Priest Poems - This is a collection of Fr. Longenecker's poems. Written in traditional forms but with a contemporary voice, Fr. Longenecker meditates on spiritual images alive in the ordinary life of a priest. Each poem is a little window into a new way of seeing reality. Each page shows the reader a fresh way of connecting with God's light and love alive in the ordinary world.

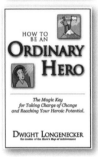

How to Be an Ordinary Hero is a short book that explains the personal growth program Dwight devised and taught in the business training company he started before he was ordained as a priest. This simple story follows the hero named Harry as he goes on his own hero's quest and learns how to become an "Ordinary Hero". This is a great book for children and teens, and everyone can benefit from the simple wisdom about life's journey.

Follow Fr Longenecker's well known blog *Standing on My Head* by connecting through his website: dwightlongenecker.com. Through the website you can also subscribe to his weekly newsletter *Faith Works!* which provides short, practical advice on living the Catholic faith.

Fr. Longenecker also writes regularly for *The National Catholic Register, CRUX, Imaginative Conservative, ZENIT, Aleteia* and other websites. He is a popular and dynamic speaker on a variety of topics. Why not connect through his website and invite him to lead your parish mission, retreat or recommend him to your local conference organizers? Through the website you can also listen to Fr Longenecker's weekly homilies from Our Lady of the Rosary church and listen to his radio show episodes as downloadable podcasts.

BIOGRAPHY

Fr. Dwight Longenecker is an American who has spent most of his life living and working in England. After graduating from the fundamentalist Bob Jones University with a degree in Speech and English, he went to study theology at Oxford University. He was eventually ordained as an Anglican priest and served as a curate, a school chaplain in Cambridge and a country parson.

Realizing that he and the Anglican Church were on divergent paths, in 1995 Fr. Dwight and his family were received into the Catholic Church.

He spent the next ten years working as a freelance Catholic writer, contributing to over twenty-five magazines, papers and journals in Britain, Ireland and the U.S.

In 2006, Fr. Dwight returned to the United States to be ordained as a priest for the diocese of Charleston, South Carolina. This brought him and his family back not only to his hometown, but also to the American Bible Belt and the hometown of Bob Jones University.

He now serves as parish priest of Our Lady of the Rosary parish in Greenville, South Carolina.

Fr. Dwight enjoys movies, blogging, books, and visiting Benedictine monasteries. He's married to Alison. They have four children named Benedict, Madeleine, Theodore and Elias. They live in Greenville, South Carolina with assorted pets, including a black Labrador named Anna and a chocolate lab named Felicity.